way of the noodle

BOXTREE

Words by Russell Cronin

Colour images by
Michael Freeman,
using background effects
from Fresco and Terrazzo
software developed by Xaos
Tools.

Black and white photographs
by Phil Sayer, except for the
'wagabowl' picture on page
96, which is by Judah
Passow.

Design and layout by
Bradbury and Williams.

For wagamama: Akio, Alan,
Christian, Dave, David,
Debbie, Jack, Lincoln, Mory,
Pauline, Soon, Simon, Tina,
Y.C.

First published 1994 by Boxtree Limited

This edition published 1998 by Boxtree
an imprint of Pan Macmillan Ltd
Pan Macmillan, 20 New Wharf Road, London N1 9RR
Basingstoke and Oxford
Associated companies throughout the world
www.panmacmillan.com

ISBN 1 85283 998 8

Colour photography © Michael Freeman

Black-and-white photography © Phil Sayer

Photograph on page 96 © Judah Passow

10 9 8

Colour images processed by Blackjacks

Printed in Great Britain by Bath Press Colourbooks, Glasgow

A CIP catalogue entry for this book is available
from the British Library

contents

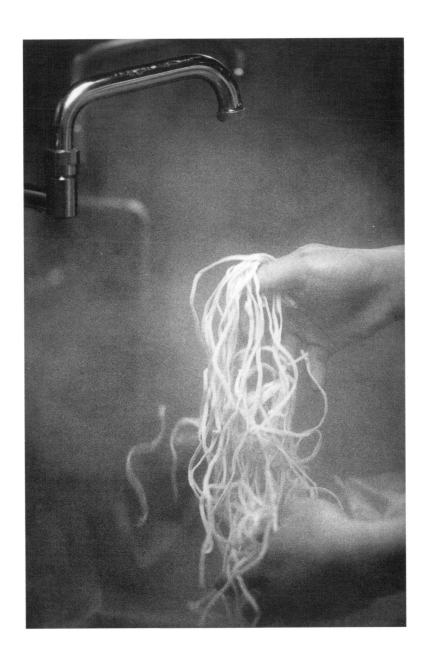

what is wagamama?

wagamama, in the Japanese vernacular, means a naughty child. Selfish and willful, the child that is said to be 'wagamama' demands constant attention and is unable to comprehend why its desires cannot be instantly gratified.

wagamama is a noodle canteen that first opened for business in Bloomsbury, central London, on 22nd April 1992, offering substantial portions of freshly-made, nutritious noodle dishes in a clean air environment at reasonable cost.

The purpose of wagamama is to feed the people; the intention of this book is to instruct the people to feed themselves.

positive eating + positive living

food intelligence = open mouths + open minds

It pays to be fussy about your food, for how wisely it is said that we are what we eat. Buddhists believe that with our thoughts we make our world and that a man is nothing more than the sum of the food that he puts into his body and the thoughts that occur in his mind. Therefore it is vital to think good thoughts and, especially when thinking about food, to think positive.

Physiology and psychology are inextricably intertwined, so that if a man eats nothing but pork, he will eventually come to resemble a pig and behave like a pig and think piggish thoughts. Only by consuming a properly-balanced diet can this poor, porcine person hope to know himself truly as a rounded human being.

Ancient Taoist philosophy teaches that the proper purpose of human life is the search for harmony and that all sickness is the manifestation of discord. Buddhists strive to maintain the symbiosis of yin and yang, the opposing but complementary forces of nature that may be characterised as dark and light, male and female, acid and alkali.

In dietary terms, this philosophy dictates that if you must eat pork, which is strongly yin, then you must also ingest a proportionately larger quantity of something yang: apples, perhaps. Not that a correct Buddhist could contemplate eating a dead pig in the first place.

The most pure example of this balanced approach to food preparation is to be found in the shojin cuisine prepared in Zen Buddhist temples, where cooking is a devotional discipline intended to improve the pupils' training and practice of the Buddhist faith. The ideogram representing the word 'shojin' is composed of the characters for 'spirit' and 'to progress'; its literal meaning is 'assiduous effort'. Only the most zealous monks are permitted to work in the kitchen, for the aim of Zen cookery is to elevate the most humble vegetarian ingredients into food fit for the most enlightened of men.

This most positive way of eating was introduced to the West by George Ohsawa, who became interested in Zen cookery not through a quest for spiritual enlightenment but through his search for physical good health. He investigated the scientifically-sound principles underlying the traditions of shojin and, in order to explain it in the West, used the adjective macrobiotic. The word comes from the Greek: 'makros', meaning 'long' and 'bios' meaning 'life'.

Modern science has yet to fully comprehend the complex biochemistry of our bodies. So far, nutritionists have a range of at least 40 vitamins, minerals and amino acids, which act synergistically and are essential for preserving good health and fitness. New discoveries are constantly being made about the particular value of individual nutrients, but it has long been apparent that our well-being greatly depends on the quality and verity of what we take in as food.

Positive eating simply means thinking carefully about everything you put into your mouth. By consciously feeding your body with the sustenance it needs to function most efficiently, you will maximise the potential energy obtained from your food, increase your stamina and begin to build an indomitable physiology, so that you are truly fit to face the rigours of life.

As soon as you start to eat properly, you will find that your thinking becomes clearer. By considering the nutritional value of everything you eat, you will start to lose any lingering desire for non-essential or so-called 'junk' foods. Soon you will come to recognise cravings for – let's say – chocolate as nothing more meaningful than a temporary imbalance in your system.

convenience is the problem

Twentieth century medicine has almost eradicated widespread disease, but not all illness can be cured with pharmaceutical drugs, or the most advanced surgical techniques. Cancer, cardiovascular problems, respiratory disorders, diabetes, arthritis and depression are all endemic in our society.

Statistics show that we are not getting any healthier. Sadly, some of us may have come to accept sicknesses caused by atmospheric pollution and stress as an unfortunate but unavoidable side-effect of modern life. But, while it may not be possible to dodge every 'flu virus that goes around, we can make ourselves more resilient by nurturing our immune system. Although we cannot always control our external environment, we are in charge of our own bodies and can easily dictate what goes on inside us by the simple expedient of taking care over how and what we eat so that our bodies' defence mechanisms can withstand any but the most virulent attack.

Comparative surveys have identified the typical British diet as being one of the poorest in the developed world, leading to chronic health problems. Nearly a quarter of the population dies unnecessarily, from preventable diseases, as a consequence of having lived on packaged, processed foods that are full of sugar and ooze hydrogenated fats. In Britain today, people's arteries are furring up so fast that somebody has a heart attack every three minutes as a direct result of negative eating habits.

The situation is so serious that the Government has formulated an initiative called *The Health of the Nation*. It aims to lower the level of fats in the national diet to within target parameters by the end of the century, but contains no statutory requirement for the food industry to take action. Instead, the more enlightened manufacturers are committed to doing good by stealth: gradually reducing the saturated fats, sugar and salt contained in their products without compromising their flavour.

This discreet approach to promoting better health assumes that the average consumer is incapable of making an informed choice when presented with the facts. Indeed, many people believe that they are confused by contradictory information from nutritionists who cannot seem to agree about what exactly constitutes the ideal diet.

In reality, there is a strong consensus. The perfect diet is high in fibre and low in fat, with plenty of vitamins and minerals and little protein. Our parents' generation used to think of good food in terms of 'square meals', but it is now apparent that the most healthy diet can best be explained by way of a food pyramid. Imagine the broad base of the pyramid is filled with the kind of complex carbohydrates found in rice, bread, potatoes, pasta and noodles, foods which should form the bulk of your daily diet. The next largest category – and level two of the pyramid – consists of vitamin and mineral-rich fruits and vegetables; above that is a smaller quantity of protein-rich foods, then a tiny quantity of fats and sugars at the apex.

eschew processed food products

Modern life is hectic and, too often, our choice of food is dictated not by a desire for good health, but by convenience. People who believe they are pressed for time take ready-made meals from the freezer and reheat them in the microwave. The problem with frozen pizza and oven-ready chips is that those foods have had most of their natural goodness stripped from them and a range of artificial chemicals added to prolong shelf life, preserve texture, and enhance flavour.

Fast food is frequently called 'junk' food because it has little or no nutritional value. The simple carbohydrates typically found in highly processed foods are practically pure sugar; they can be burnt in the body for a quick burst of energy but the calories they provide are nutritionally hollow. Consequently, many young people who consume too much pre-cooked takeaway food and artificially sweetened soft drinks have been found to suffer from dramatic mood swings and sometimes violent urges.

Rationally, we recognise that junk food that is saturated with sleazy calories cannot be good for us, but still we might be tempted to eat it when we cannot be bothered to put together a proper meal. However, as soon as we cease to think of food merely as a sop to our pangs of hunger and start to pay proper attention to nutrition, we begin to realise that junk food is not worth eating.

Noodles are most familiar in the West in the form of dehydrated snacks that can be prepared almost instantaneously with the addition of boiling water. Instant noodles – cup ramen – have been popular in Japan since the processing technique was invented in the 1950s and there are now a bewildering

profusion of varieties on the market. Sociologists have seen these ersatz noodles as a distressing symbol of the destruction of traditional Japanese culture, but in reality they pose no threat to the ramen bars that have flourished throughout the country for the past 200 years.

Proper noodles and a good soup stock do, of course, take some time and skill to make from scratch but, once the components are prepared, a bowl of ramen soup can be assembled and served within minutes. Ramen offers a nutritionally complete meal in a bowl: the noodles, containing valuable carbohydrate and dietary fibre, swim in a healthful broth and are topped with vitamin-rich vegetables, plus a little protein in the form of meat, seafood or tofu, and minimum fat.

oriental table manners

In stark contrast to the grim Western diet, the Japanese way of eating approaches the harmonious ideal. Its fundamental principles are freshness and natural purity, closely followed by aesthetic appeal. Good food should satisfy all the senses, but the Japanese eat first with their eyes. A formal meal consists of a series of exquisite dishes that are as beautiful as they are delicious.

Portions are small so that one never feels stuffed, for, as a Japanese proverb says, 'leaving the table hungry is the basis of good health'. Another maxim we like at wagamama is 'an empty stomach is the prerequisite of any creative activity'. Meditate on this thought for a moment: we love food but we value hunger.

Japanese culture was born of austerity and, over centuries, the people have learned how to make the most of the resources that are available to

the first task of the
day is to wash the
face of wagamama
and to sweep the
pavement outside.

deliveries of fresh
supplies soon start
to arrive, down the
back stairs and
straight into the
kitchen.

uncluttered interior
design enhances the
utilitarian purpose
of wagamama.

them. The islands of Japan are too small and too crowded to be able to spare vast tracts of pasture for grazing cattle and sheep, but they are surrounded by seas full of fish. Even if fish does not play an obvious part in a Japanese meal, it will usually be present in the form of the staple cooking stock, called dashi, which is made using flakes shaved from a dried fillet of bonito, a fish of the mackerel family, and a species of seaweed called konbu (giant kelp).

Seaweed is rarely eaten in the West, but is the richest natural source of organic mineral salts – especially calcium, iron, magnesium and zinc – and it contains almost no calories. Seaweed is also rich in iodine and selenium, both of which have proven medicinal qualities. Apart from konbu, the most common varieties of seaweed used in Japanese cookery are nori, which is used to wrap sushi, and wakame, which is used in soups.

The traditional Japanese diet contains very little animal fat and no dairy products, which in the West are promoted as indispensible sources of protein. Protein is necessary for children to grow and for adults to rebuild worn muscle tissue, but it is the most complex of food elements and the most difficult to digest.

There is an enduring myth that eating animal protein gives us energy, but the truth is quite the reverse. Cows' milk is intended to feed calves, not human beings, and adults find dairy products particularly difficult to digest. Meat is so hard for our bodies to break down that it actually robs us of energy. That is why, after a big roast dinner we are liable to feel more than a little lazy.

What is more, the protein found in milk and meat cannot be readily utilised by our bodies and it comes weighted with undesirable saturated fats. In fact, the only good reason for eating meat and cheese is if you like the way they taste. Consequently, it's advisable to treat these foodstuffs as luxuries, to be enjoyed only once in a while. If it is protein you are after, far better to seek it, as the Japanese do, from soy.

nature's miracle protein

Soybeans are also known as 'the meat of the fields', since they yield more protein per land unit than any other grain or legume. Chemically, the composition of soybeans is closer to that of peanuts than other beans and soy is nutritionally superior among vegetable proteins since it contains a full set of essential amino acids. Also, the unsaturated fat in soybeans is the kind that has been shown to inhibit heart disease, which is encouraged by animal fats.

Soybeans are practically indigestible in their raw state, but the Chinese pioneered various methods of processing them in order to extract their goodness. They may be milled, mixed with water, and the slurry boiled and strained to make soy milk. This can be drunk as a beverage or made into a curd called tofu. The beans can be soaked, boiled and fermented into a paste called miso.

The extraordinary medicinal power of miso was first postulated by Dr Shinchiro Akizuki, who spent much of his career treating victims of the atomic bomb that was dropped on Nagasaki at the end of World War Two. Although they worked just a few miles from the epicentre of the bomb blast, neither he nor his colleagues suffered from the usual effects of radiation because, Dr Akizuki claimed, they drank miso soup every day.

In 1972, his theory was confirmed when researchers discovered that miso contains dipicolonic acid, an alkaloid that counteracts the effect of heavy metals, such as radioactive strontium, and helps discharge them from the body.

culinary acculturation

The techniques of processing soybeans are but one aspect of Chinese cuisine and culture that the Japanese adopted and refined to make their own. Japanese tofu is softer, whiter and more delicately-flavoured that the Chinese variety and Japanese soy sauce is thinner, lighter in colour, and sweeter to taste. Noodles, too, were a Chinese invention that has been thoroughly assimilated into the Japanese way of life.

Rice is the staple food of Japan, but it was not until comparatively recently that rice cultivation began to spread throughout the country. More common, especially in the southern regions, were grains that could be ground into flour and made into dough. Rather than bake bread, however, the Japanese sliced the dough into strips that could be boiled in a pot, as they had learned from the Chinese.

The starchy dough from which noodles (and all types of pasta) are made is universally acknowledged to be a primary source of sustained energy. Many of today's top athletes train on a diet composed almost exclusively of pasta, together with salads and barely-cooked vegetables. The wheatflour from which pasta is usually made is a good source of complex carbohydrate, which the body can burn most easily to provide energy.

Pasta also contains a good quantity of the kind of fibre that is necessary for effective digestion and efficient elimination of waste from the bowels. Insoluble fibre absorbs the food waste that the body does not require which may then be effortlessly excreted. The buckwheat flour from which soba noodles are made has long been recognised as being particularly valuable in this respect.

In one of the earliest known Japanese books, the *Honch Shoku Kan* (Food Dictionary), published in 1697, it is written that 'buckwheat is sweet, contains no poison, relaxes the nerves, eases irritability, and helps to clear out and release old faeces from the stomach and intestines.'

degenerate diet = declining health

Although the traditional Japanese diet has great nutritional integrity, over the past 50 years the Japanese have become accustomed to consuming increasing quantities of meats, eggs, and dairy products. We know precisely how much more of these foods the average person eats because every year since 1946, the Japanese Government has conducted a National Nutritional Survey, asking detailed questions of thousands of randomly-selected people about their eating habits. The results make it possible to closely monitor the correlation between dietary changes and chronic disease.

At an academic workshop organised by the International Union Against Cancer, held at Nagoya in 1989, a series of studies were presented to demonstrate how changing eating habits have influenced the incidence of cancer in the Japanese population. Since the end of World War Two, the average intake of fat has increased by 314% and animal protein by 234%, while carbohydrate and vegetable protein have both significantly decreased.

The incidence of cancer has increased proportionately.

The coincidence of a decline in the nutritional value of the national diet with an increase in cancer does not necessarily prove diet to be a causal factor in the development of disease. However, the Japanese statistics add to a mass of evidence from studies conducted around the world, indicating that daily consumers of meats are at a higher risk of developing cancers. Daily consumers of green vegetables are at lower risk of all types of cancer.

The reduction of risk from lung cancer by eating fresh vegetables every day is, unsurprisingly, most apparent among heavy cigarette smokers who put themselves at risk from the adverse effects of free radicals. Free radicals are biochemical rogues that gang up in the body to vandalise cells and do the sort of damage that leads to cancer. They are formed as a reaction to atmospheric pollution and are most common in cigarette smoke. They are best combatted by the 'antioxidant' vitamins that are abundant in fresh fruits and vegetables.

vigilante vitamins

The principal antioxidants are vitamins C and E and vitamin A, which the body makes from beta carotene, a natural plant dye that was first identified in carrots. Dark green leafy vegetables like spinach and broccoli also contain a lot of beta carotene and they would be orange, too, if they didn't also contain chlorophyll. Beta carotene is just one of the miraculous natural chemicals found in raw food that are so easily denatured by cooking.

The application of heat to food rapidly changes its molecular structure and destroys its essential goodness. Overcooked food is often described as having had 'the life cooked out of it', and 'done to death'. You do not want to eat dead food! Rather, food should be cooked as briefly as possible and eaten as close to its raw state as is palatable.

When cooking meat or fish, it is better to grill than to fry or roast. The heat of the grill will sear the outside of the flesh and seal in its flavour and most of its juices without adding extra calories in the form of fat, or allowing all the juices to escape. Blanching vegetables in boiling water literally dissolves vitamins, particularly vitamin C and those of the B group. It is better to steam vegetables, since steam is hotter than boiling water and does not leach out minerals and enzymes in the process. Stir-frying is also a good method of cooking to retain goodness. When making ramen soups use such toppings as mushrooms, beansprouts and manges touts in their crunchy, raw state.

The life-enhancing effects of eating a diet high in raw, uncooked fruits and vegetables were well known by the ancient cultures and have been demonstrated countless times in the most modern health clinics. Scientists are now coming to recognise that the root cause of much chronic illness lies in the imbalance of sodium and potassium in cooked food, particularly if it has been grown using chemical fertilisers and pesticides.

Sodium and potassium are essential minerals that act as nutritional antagonists, working synergistically within the body. Sodium is found in extracellular fluids such as blood plasma, while potassium is present inside cells. The two opposing minerals maintain an osmotic pressure on the walls of each cell, keeping it strong. When an imbalance occurs and there is too much sodium, or not enough potassium in the system, the biochemical effects can be disastrous.

there is much to be done before lunchtime; it's all hands to the pump.

meanwhile, a queue of hungry people begins to form before the door is opened.

as high noon approaches, activity becomes focused on the service ahead, during which the kitchen will dispense a bowl of ramen every 23 seconds.

This recent scientific hypothesis would come as no revelation to a Buddhist monk. Since sodium is yang and potassium yin, it should be obvious that the balance between the two must be carefully maintained if one is to preserve good health.

raw power

Raw energy is the astonishing rejuvenating power contained within uncooked fruits and vegetables that scientists are not yet able to properly explain. A chemist might attribute it to the volatility of enzymes, which have been described as the body's 'spark plugs', and the high redox potential of elements like vitamin C, which promote optimal electron exchange and make living tissue positively fizz!

The most effective way to consume fruit and vegetables is in the form of raw juice, which wagamama always recommends to its customers. Freshly-extracted juice is the most efficient food. Being mostly water, it is rapidly absorbed and has the effect of cleansing and nurturing the system as it is being digested. Fresh juice is the richest natural source of minerals, vitamins and enzymes, all of which neutralise toxins and boost the body's immune system.

To experience the benefits of drinking fresh juices, unless you are lucky to live next door to a juice bar, you will have to buy yourself a juicer. Store-bought juice is not as good as real fresh juice, because it will usually have been pasteurised and exposed to heat in the packaging process, which destroys much of its goodness.

Once you own a juicer and get into the habit of using it every day, you can stop taking any other dietary supplements, since a glass of raw juice is far better for you than the biggest synthetic vitamin pill. The best time to drink juice is in the morning, on an empty stomach, when the juice will be absorbed most rapidly into your system and its essential nutrients can be most readily absorbed.

Some people (and some books) will advise you that fruit and vegetable juices should not be combined. It is true that those with impaired digestion, food allergies, or chronic fatigue who are trying to detoxify themselves with raw juices can benefit from not mixing them. For those of us who are not so delicate, however, the worst that can happen when we mix live fruit and vegetable juices in the same glass is that we may experience some flatulence. It is undeniably true that some juice combinations can make you fart, but do not let that inhibit you! It is important that you consume the juices of as wide a variety of fruits and vegetables as possible and the combinations you choose to take them in are purely a matter of personal preference, so allow your taste buds to be your guide.

At wagamama we do not like rules, but here are three basic guidelines for good juicing:

★ Some juices – broccoli or beetroot, for instance – are too strong to drink straight. Dilute them with water or with other, blander vegetable juices like cucumber and celery.

★ Apple and carrot juices are most useful because they combine well with any other juice. Use them as a basis for experimentation.

★ When juicing citrus fruit, leave on most of the white pith as this contains bioflavinoids which counteract acidity of the fruit and help digestion.

use your noodle

At wagamama we believe that good health should not be defined merely as the absence of disease, but as a dynamic condition in which we feel optimistic, energetic and fully alive. We think that the quality of your life is greatly determined by the quality of your food, by the choices you make about what you consume.

Everything you put into your body must either be assimilated or eliminated. For the body to function efficiently, it must be fuelled with the kind of wholesome foodstuffs that will tend to cleanse and nurture the system, not clog it with toxins. While it is important to have a working knowledge of nutrition, do not make a big deal out of it. Nutrition by numbers, involving obsessive calorie counting and eccentric food combinations, is not only boring but it offers no guarantee of good health and is almost certain to make you unhappy.

Dieting to lose weight is not a long term strategy for good health; the very concept implies a short-term regime. When you have starved yourself down to your target weight, you will revert to your old eating habits and soon start to gain again. Instead, you must examine your eating patterns and eliminate negative practices or at least be aware that some of the things you eat purely for pleasure are not going to give you anything in terms of sustenance. Healthy eating should then become a way of life.

Find out all you need to learn about nutrition and then forget it. Positive eating should become a subconscious action and it is enough to have at the back of your mind the thought that food is the very stuff of life and diet is the primary means by which an individual determines his or her destiny. Eating

well is the key to all human social activity, culture and civilisation. But don't get uptight about it! Rather, relax and learn to listen to what your body tells you it needs. Learn to trust your appetite and try to eat instinctively, whatever you feel like.

Finally, do not be slovenly at the table, but cultivate correct table manners. Sit with a good posture and take a moment before you begin eating to express gratitude, inwardly or out loud, for your food. No matter how hungry you are, do not gobble, but chew each mouthful thoroughly before swallowing. Drink only moderately while eating, so as not to dilute the digestive juices.

Most importantly, pay attention to what you are putting into your mouth. Appreciate its appearance, aroma, texture and flavour by all means, but first you must examine your food critically and ask yourself, 'How much good is this going to do me?'

way of the noodle

birth of the noodle

'Noodles,' according to the early Chinese historian, Shu Hsi, 'were mainly an invention of the common people.' Chinese peasants first found out how to make noodles sometime during the first century BC, soon after they got their hands on grain mills, which enabled them to grind wheat into flour.

Quickly these commoners learned how to add water to the flour and knead the mixture to make dough, which could then be rolled out and cut into noodles or, with practice, extruded by hand. It was not long before the first street noodle sellers had set up their stalls, and by the end of the Han period, even the Emperor was eating noodles.

At this time, the Japanese had no written language and had yet to learn how to eat using chopsticks. Both of these skills they acquired from the Chinese. As far as writing is concerned, the Chinese system was adopted but the characters were found to be inadequate in expressing the subtleties of the Japanese language. Therefore, a system of phonetic modifications was developed for use in conjunction with the Chinese pictograms, to create an entirely distinctive way of writing.

Similarly, the Chinese invented the process of making bean curd but the Japanese refined the techniques to enhance both the texture and flavour of tofu, creating an entirely new sub-genre of cookery. In the same way, once the techniques of noodle-making had been introduced to Japan during the Heian period (794–1185), they were swiftly assimilated into the developing Japanese cuisine.

indigenous noodles

Japanese noodles, or menrui, fall into two distinct categories: the wheat-based noodles associated with Osaka and the more fertile south of the country, and noodles made with buckwheat which are more common in the cooler northern regions around Tokyo. There are many varieties of noodle, but most typical are the fat white noodles made with wheat flour, called udon, and the thinner, brownish ones made with buckwheat, called soba.

Monks who travelled to China for their training were the first to learn how to make noodles and the temples became the first places in Japan where noodles were served. A monk called Genkei, writing in the Muromachi period (1394–1596) mentions udon and its more refined cousin, somen. Very slender, like vermicelli, somen are the only type of noodle considered fine enough to be used in the rigorous shojin cuisine of Zen monasteries.

The earliest mention of soba noodles occurs in the diaries of a priest called Jisho. On 3rd February 1614, Jisho recorded that he paid a visit to the Jomyo Temple in old Edo (now Tokyo) and was offered a bowl of noodles made with buckwheat. Soba was, it seems, served to all visitors who came to pay their respects to departed relatives — until word spread of the excellence of these noodles and crowds of bogus mourners began turning up at the temple to claim their free soba.

urban noodles

During the early years of the 17th Century, labourers were pouring in from all over the country to assist in the construction of the new capital city, Edo. In this bustling atmosphere, where three quarters of the population were men, a simple and satisfying meal of noodles provided a quick source of energy and soon the first street stalls selling soba started to spring up.

Sometime between 1711 and 1726, a crude version of kake soba, hot noodles in broth, was served at a venerable old noodle shop called Shinano, which still exists in what is now the Shinjuku-ku quarter of downtown Tokyo. Unlike the noodle soup dishes of today, which must be hot, this early version was served at room temperature, with lukewarm broth being poured over pre-cooked noodles. No doubt the hard-working labourers on this new frontier did not have time to wait for their food to cool before consuming it.

A clue to the rough-and-ready nature of the early noodle shops can be surmised from historical references to yotaka, or 'nighthawk', soba. As the hawk remains active after dark, so the noodle stalls in the red light district of Yoshiwara stayed open late into the evening. Not only did they offer fast food, but they also provided an opportunity for prostitutes to pick up passing trade. They would call out to potential customers, 'chotto, chotto...' ('just a minute'), a cry which somewhat resembles the cry of a hawk. Consequently, the whores and the noodle sellers got stuck with the same label.

say no to noodle snobs

In 1726 a board in the Kanda district of old Edo advertised 'two eight instant kendon noodles.' Kendon is a word used to describe behaviour that is coarse or loud and was also applied to the cheapest and most common whores, the ones that called out most noisily to passers-by in the street. Whatever the significance of the words 'two eight,' we can assume that there was very little ceremony associated with the service of kendon noodles.

Edo culture reached its peak in the second half of the 18th Century with a period of conspicuous consumption that bordered on decadence. Social distinctions became blurred as the common people lost respect for and began to ridicule their betters, while it became fashionable among the aristocracy to ape the lower classes. It became iki — chic — to eat at humble noodle stalls, but to do so in contemplative silence. This snobbish affectation only had the effect of encouraging the commoners to slurp their noodles even more noisily.

As noodles and noodle shops became more sophisticated, the true connoisseur preferred them to be served with hardly any broth or with a dipping sauce, so that the delicate flavour of the noodles could be savoured. Slurping noodles in broth came to be seen as the sign that the eater was a country bumpkin, unused to the civilised ways of the big city. Eventually, these sloppy street noodles came to be known as da-soba, junk food, and no self-respecting noodle afficionado would patronise the humble kendon joints that served them.

The rakugo masters, raconteurs who entertained the people with comic monologues that drew philosophical conclusions from the ordinary events of everyday life, adopted the noodle as a metaphor in their stories. One classic tale concerns a cultured noodle connoisseur, the kind of elitist gourmet who would patronise only the most sophisticated noodle shops. Only on his deathbed does this lifelong noodle snob recant, his final wish being to enjoy a hearty bowl of noodles, country fashion, swimming in broth.

the rise of ramen

Udon and soba are now so thoroughly assimilated into traditional culture that it is doubtful whether any contemporary Japanese ever consider their Chinese origin. However, the threadlike noodles bound with egg, called ramen, flaunt their Chinese roots. Ramen literally means 'Chinese-style noodle' and was a comparatively recent import to Japan. Enterprising Chinese noodle peddlars began setting up ramen shops in Tokyo only during the last century.

By 1818 there were already some 6,000 noodle shops in Tokyo and the shrewd Chinese entrepreneurs, when they set up the first ramen shops, cunningly imitated the conventions of rival establishments, copying their interior design and even hanging the same signs. It is, perhaps, for this reason that several ramen dishes were historically mis-named: a couple of the most popular dishes at wagamama – yaki soba and moyashi soba – are actually made using ramen noodles.

So effective were the proprietors of these ramen shops that nowadays many younger Japanese probably do not know the difference between the indigenous udon and soba noodles and the upstart ramen. The situation is further confused by the cheap Chinese-style restaurants, called Chuka Ryori-Ya, which offer popular Chinese dishes including ramen, but are usually run by Japanese people. Authentic Chinese restaurants would never stoop so low as to serve street food and, if noodles are to be found on their menus at all, they will be hand-thrown.

Noodles are now ubiquitous throughout Japan and ramen bars are to be found everywhere from suburban street corners to railway station platforms, where commuters hurriedly eat on their way to or from work. Each has its own speciality, usually restricting the menu to only two or three of the countless permutations of ramen soup dishes that exist, and will usually conform to the style that is characteristic of the region: the soup base of

Tokyo ramen is salty and has much soy, while that of Osaka is lighter and more refined.

The Kyushu-style ramen has a broth base of thick, white pork stock and the Hokkaido-style, made famous by the Sapporoya ramen franchise chain, is lip-smackingly spicy.

the correct way to eat noodles

There are many ways to serve ramen, but only one way to eat noodle soups and that is with maximum gusto. You must suck trailing noodles up between your lips, for it may be bad luck to break them with your teeth. You must smack your lips to show proper appreciation. Above all, you must slurp the soup as noisily as possible.

The most sensible explanation for this ritual is that the slurping oxygenates the hot soup and cools it so as not to scald the roof of the mouth, as it is the number one prerequisite for a correctly-served bowl of ramen that the soup must be boiling hot. Still, there really is no practical reason for making such a noise, except to show enjoyment.

wagapopo

'people who eat noodles are all amateurs.'

TAMPOPO

Juzo Itami described his film, *Tampopo* ('Dandelion') as a 'ramen western' (as opposed to a spaghetti western). Its hero is a trucker called Goro, who wears a low-brimmed hat and an impassive expression. As he drives through the night, his mate, Gun, reads aloud:

'One fine day, I went out with an old man. He'd studied noodles for 40 years. He was showing me the right way to eat them...'

At the counter of a noodle shop, the young narrator of the tale grabs his bowl as soon as it is served and dives greedily into it . Then, noticing that his companion had not moved, he asks:

'Master... Soup first or noodles first?'

'First,' the wise old man tells him, 'observe the whole bowl.
Appreciate its gestalt, savour the aromas.
Jewels of fat glittering on the surface.
Shinachiku roots shining.
Seaweed slowly sinking.
Spring onions floating.
Concentrate on the three pork slices,' he instructs his student. 'They play the key role, but stay modestly hidden.'

Taking up his chopsticks, the wise old man continues:

'Caress the surface with the chopstick tips to express affection. Then poke the pork; just touch it. Stroke it affectionately with the tips of the chopsticks. Then gently pick it up and dip it into the soup on the right of the bowl. What's important here is to apologise to the pork by saying, "see you soon".

'Finally, start eating, the noodles first. At this time, while slurping the noodles, look at the pork.'

The fascinated young man watched as the old man bit some shinachiku root and chewed it awhile. Still chewing noodles, he took some more shinachiku. Then he sipped some soup, three times. He sat up, sighed, picked up one slice of pork as if making a major decision in life and lightly tapped it on the side of the bowl.

'What for?' asks the young acolyte of his Master, anxiously.

The sensei smiles serenely and says, 'To drain it, that's all.'

the noodle apprentice

This tale makes Goro and Gun hungry for noodles so they stop at a humble ramen shop – a naruto and nori type – called *Lai Lai*, which the widow Tampopo has been struggling to run on her own since her husband died, with no one to help her save her young son, Tabu.

Inside, Gun immediately notices that the water in which Tampopo is cooking her noodles is not boiling. A bad sign. Later, when Tampopo asks for their honest opinion of her noodles, Goro tries to be diplomatic, telling her that 'they've got sincerity, but they lack guts...'

'Frankly,' says Gun, 'they're bad.'

As they leave, Tampopo runs out to the truck to ask Goro, 'Please be my teacher. Please. I'll be a good student. Meeting you makes me want to become a real noodle cook. For my son, too. I'll do anything,' she begs. 'So please, please teach me.'

Reluctantly at first, Goro agrees and the training begins with Tampopo lugging a pot full of water from one side of the kitchen to the other in order to build her muscles. With a stopwatch, Goro checks how long it takes her to prepare and serve half a dozen bowls of noodles. He tells her that she must be faster; she must beat three minutes.

Goro takes Tampopo on a tour of the local noodle shops, to observe what makes a good place. At the first, only the welcome from the cooks has real clout. They chatter too much and there is much wasted motion. At the next shop, however, two older cooks work together silently, harmoniously, and well.

'This is a good place,' says Goro. 'The customers feel good, too. See? They keep drinking the soup down to the last drop. Look when they return their bowls. Watch closely. The old man looks at every empty bowl to see if the soup is finished. It's the soup that animates the noodles; that's why he checks so carefully.'

life is a noodle; zen is the soup in which it is suspended

Noodles are the heart of a bowl of ramen, but the soul of the bowl is the soup. In the wagamama kitchen, we say that 'soup is everything'. Since the success of your ramen dishes will depend to a great extent on the quality of your soup, it's important to understand the principles of making stocks with meat and fish bones and without them.

In the movie, Tampopo goes to great lengths to get a good recipe, even paying the owner of the premises adjacent to a noodle shop that serves a half decent soup to allow her to spy through a crack in the wall as the ingredients are being put into the stockpot. In reality, there is no mystery to making good soup stocks. One must carefully follow a few simple procedures.

Nonetheless, getting it right turns into a nightmare for Tampopo, literally. Eventually, Goro has to take her to ask the advice of the old Master, the king of a tribe of gourmet vagabonds, who eat from the dustbins of only the finest restaurants. In the park where they meet, Goro introduces him to Tampopo: 'This is our Master. He was a doctor. While he was selling noodles for fun, his partner stole his wife and practice. Now he's our resident gourmet.'

'Let's review the basic rules of soup,' says the Master. 'Fowl spoils quickly, so use only the freshest chicken. Both chicken and pork have strong smells, so parboil them first and then rinse them well in cold water. Don't cut the vegetables. The main point is heat. Heat releases the soul of the ingredients.'

The Master heats his stockpot rapidly but he never allows it to come to a full boil for, as he tells Tampopo, 'If you boil it, the soup will never be clear. And keep skimming the scum off.'

For his demonstration of how to make stock, the Master has what he calls 'a most interesting addition' to that day's stock: a pig's head! Holding it up for Tampopo to inspect, he says, 'Isn't he wonderful?' Horrified, Tampopo faints away.

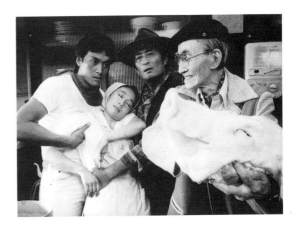

how to make ramen soups

Like Tampopo, we at wagamama are not so fond of pork, preferring a lighter, chicken-based stock. It is always worth buying a whole chicken, rather than packaged pieces of breast or leg, so that you can use the carcass for making stock. We do like to put some pork bones into the stockpot, to add colour and body to the soup, but not too many.

The stockpot must be capacious, even if you are cooking only for yourself, with a capacity of at least three litres, although five litres would be better. Unless you have a stockpot of industrial dimensions, it will sadly be necessary to contravene the Master's instructions and to cut the vegetables into chunks. Any mild green vegetables can be added to the stock, but we prefer the broad-leaved Chinese leaves which impart a subtle sweetness.

basic ramen soup stock

ingredients

a chicken carcass
some pork bones
an onion
a couple of carrots
some celery stalks
a head of Chinese leaves

method

★ Put the chicken carcass into the pot, breaking it into smaller pieces if necessary, and cover with cold water. Quickly bring the water to the boil and, as soon as it does boil, turn off the heat, drain off the water and pour it away. The bones will be clean enough to start!

★ Add the vegetables to the washed bones in the stockpot, chopping them roughly if necessary.

Cover with cold water and turn up the heat to bring it almost to the boil as quickly as possible. Remember that the stock must not be allowed to come to a full boil. If it becomes necessary to rapidly reduce the heat of the stock to prevent it from doing so, pour in a glass of cold water.

★ Before the stock comes to a full boil, turn the heat down to simmer and skim off the scum that will have formed on the surface, using a spoon or a ladle.

★ Simmer the stock for at least couple of hours, watching and adjusting the heat to ensure that it keeps bubbling gently but does not boil. Periodically skim any scum from the surface.

★ After a couple of hours, when all the flavour has been extracted from the bones, strain the stock through a fine sieve.

vegetarian soup stock

This elementary vegetarian stock is very easy to make. Unlike stocks containing meat, it does not matter if the liquid in a vegetarian stock is boiled vigorously. In fact, it is essential to extract maximum flavour from the vegetables.

ingredients

an onion
a couple of carrots
a cucumber
a head of Chinese leaves
a tomato
a bay leaf

★ Roughly chop the vegetables and put them into a large stockpot with the bayleaf and the tomato.

★ Fill the pot with water and turn up the heat to bring it to the boil as quickly as possible.

★ When the water boils, turn the heat down and skim any scum from the surface.

★ Simmer the stock for at least three hours, skimming regularly, before straining.

fish soup stock

Many people make fish stock using just the bones and this is fine if you happen to be filleting a lot of fish. At wagamama, however, we like to use a whole fish, preferably a fresh red mullet. Remember to gut it thoroughly first.

ingredients

a fish
half a mouli (Oriental white radish)
a bunch of coriander
a bunch of watercress
a thumb-sized piece of ginger, finely chopped

method

★ Put all the ingredients in the stockpot and cover them with cold water.

★ Turn up the heat under the stockpot to bring it to the boil as quickly as possible.

★ When it boils, turn the heat down to simmer and skim the stock.

★ Continue to simmer, skimming regularly, for at least a couple of hours, before straining.

how to make dashi broths

Dashi is the fundamental cooking stock of Japanese cuisine, giving its most characteristic flavour. Its only ingredients are a species of seaweed called konbu (giant kelp) and flakes shaved from a fillet of dried katsuo (bonito, a fish of the mackerel family).

★ The seaweed and shaved fish are successively boiled in water to make a clear, aromatic and subtly-flavoured liquid that is ideal as a base for noodle soups.

★ The ingredients used to make ichiban (primary) dashi can be reserved to make niban (secondary) dashi, a heavier stock with a more intense flavour that is more suitable for stronger miso soups and the dipping sauces served with cold noodles. At wagamama, we refer to these staple stocks as dashi 1 and dashi 2.

★ Like many of the methods employed in a Japanese kitchen, the process of making dashi is deceptively simple. The stock can easily be spoiled by boiling either of the ingredients for too long, in which case the flavour will become overwhelming. Still, making a decent dashi is not difficult and it is the first secret of Japanese cooking, upon which the success or failure of your noodle soups will ultimately depend.

★ Many Japanese cooks these days never make dashi from scratch in the traditional way, but rely on the instant version, called dashi-no-moto. Sold either as granules, or in an infusion bag, and simply added to boiling water, these proprietory products can make an acceptable stock, but nothing beats the flavour of the real thing, freshly made.

★ Make only as much as you will need for one day, since dashi is likely to become cloudy if left to sit for more than 24 hours.

★ Naturally, the quality of your dashi will largely depend upon the quality of the ingredients used. The best konbu is harvested on the coast of the northern Japanese island of Hokkaido, where the dark olive-coloured leaves may grow more than a metre in height and up to 30 centimetres wide. The widest konbu is considered to be best for making dashi and if it expands and develops soft blisters while simmering, the flavour will be exceptionally good.

★ Konbu is usually sold in clear plastic packets, so that you can check its colour. If you have a choice, avoid buying konbu that is so dark it looks almost black. Look instead for a slightly speckled, deep olive-brown colour.

★ Do not worry about the white salt residue on the surface of the leaves; it is a sign that the seaweed has been dried naturally.

★ Never rinse or wash konbu since its fragrance is mostly contained on the surface of the leaves.

★ The finest dashi is made with fresh shavings from a dried fillet of bonito, but it is unlikely that you will be able to easily buy a whole fillet. Search instead for packets labelled hana-katcuo (flower bonito) or kezuri-bushi (shaved fillets) containing what looks like slightly pink wood shavings.

★ Make sure that you store your bonito flakes in an airtight container, because humidity will destroy their delicate flavour.

dashi 1

ingredients

1 litre cold water
30g konbu (three or four pieces, about 15cm long)
30g dried bonito flakes

method

★ Prepare the konbu by lightly wiping the surface with a clean, damp cloth, and, if necessary, break it into pieces small enough to fit into your stockpot.

★ Fill the pot with a litre of cold water and put the konbu into it. Heat the water slowly, so that it takes about 10 minutes to come to the boil. When the water starts to bubble and before it has come to a full boil, remove the konbu. Otherwise it will emit a powerful and unpleasant odour.

★ Test the surface of the cooked konbu with your thumbnail. If it is soft, sufficient flavour has been extracted. If it is tough, put it back into the stockpot and return it to the heat for a few more minutes, adding half a cup of cold water to stop the stock from boiling.

★ Remove the konbu and set it aside for use in making dashi 2.

★ Add the bonito flakes to the stockpot and return it to the heat. Bring the stock to a full boil, then remove it from the heat at once. If bonito is allowed to boil for more than a couple of seconds it will make the dashi bitter and too strong to use in clear soups.

★ Allow a couple of minutes for the bonito flakes to settle to the bottom of the stockpot and skim off any scum from the surface of the stock.

★ Filter the dashi through a fine sieve – a muslin or paper filter (a large coffee filter is good for this).

★ Save the bonito flakes for making dashi 2.

dashi 2

ingredients

konbu and bonito flakes left from making dashi 1
1½ litres cold water
15g dried bonito flakes

method

★ Put the leftover konbu and bonito flakes into a stockpot with the cold water and bring it quickly to the boil over a high flame.

★ When the liquid boils, turn down the heat and gently simmer for 15–20 minutes, to reduce its volume by a third.

★ When the stock is reduced to your satisfaction, add the remaining bonito flakes and remove the stockpot from the heat.

★ Allow the bonito flakes to settle, then strain the liquid through a fine sieve or filter.

vegetarian dashi

★ Since the highly soluble nutrients of seaweed pass into water very easily, it is not strictly necessary to subject the konbu to heat in order to extract its flavour and make a perfectly acceptable stock. Straightforward konbu dashi can be made simply by soaking the kelp overnight in cold water.

★ To make dashi by this method, use proportionately more konbu – 40 grams to one litre of water.

★ Lightly wipe the surface of the konbu leaves, put them into a bowl filled with the water, cover and leave to stand at room temperature for eight hours.

★ Mushrooms, particularly shiitake, may be added to enhance the flavour of konbu dashi, but it is not a good idea to use dried mushrooms as their flavour will be overpowering.

flavouring dashi broths

At traditional Japanese noodle shops, dashi broths are flavoured with a mixture of shoyu and mirin (sweet sake used for cooking) with salt and sugar, sometimes boiled up with dashi 2 and left for several days to allow the flavour of the mixture to mature. Each noodle master has his own peculiar preferences and personal theories on how long a mixture should be boiled and exactly what proportion of flavour base should be added to the dashi to make the perfect broth.

At wagamama, we prefer not to add excess salt and sugar to our recipes, but simply to mix soy sauce, or tamari, and mirin at a ratio of roughly three to two, and add the mixture to the dashi immediately before serving. The exact proportions of flavour base to dashi will depend on individual taste, but the ideal is about two tablespoons of mirin and three of shoyu per litre of dashi.

'we just make noodles in a normal way.'

GORO, *TAMPOPO*

Back in the movie *Tampopo*, Goro and Gun, the Master and Tampopo visit a refined traditional Japanese noodle shop where they order 14 portions of mori soba (cold buckwheat noodles served in a basket) between them. As they wait to be served, an old man comes into the shop supported by his young wife, who reminds him of what his doctor says he must not eat before leaving him there while she goes shopping.

Of course, the greedy old man ignores her advice completely, ordering all his favourite dishes and gobbling them down as quickly as he can. When he chokes on his tempura soba, Tampopo and her friends come to his aid, using a vacuum cleaner to unblock his oesophagus.

To show his gratitude, the old man offers them the services of his factotum, Shohei who, as a youngster, was taught to make noodles by the master of his local noodle shop.

'When you make noodles,' Shohei tells Tampopo, 'you must have a precise recipe. An exact combination of different flours, kneadings, everything.'

Together, they go to a shop that serves superb noodles.

'So smooth,' comments Shohei, 'but with great body.'

'You're right,' says Tampopo. 'Noodles can be so different.'

'To make noodles this smooth they must do an extra rolling,' Shohei knows. 'They probably let the dough sit before rolling it, but the key question is, for how long? The soda water may be a bit different too,' he adds.

'Well,' says Tampopo slyly, 'let's ask.'

She questions the cook closely, saying she found his noodles a bit different today, not quite up to the usual standard. The Chinese cook is indignant. He tells her as he made them in exactly the same way as he always does, by leaving the dough to sit overnight before rolling it three times.

'Oh,' says Tampopo, 'then perhaps it was the water that was different?'

'No,' replies the proud cook. 'I used number one Chinese spring water from my home province of Guangxi, as usual.'

'Really,' says the wily Tampopo. 'Then maybe it was just me.'

Although the basic recipe for ramen is simple and the method of making noodles is straightforward, there are a number of variables that complicate the process. Of paramount importance is the quality of the flour, which must be fresh. Egg is used to bind the dough, but the soda water that is mixed with the flour crucially affects the texture of the noodles.

Originally the mountain spring water used to make ramen was imported from China, but these days it is possible to buy mineral salts that can be added to plain tap water in the rough proportions of 600 – 800 grams per 18 litres of water. The exact amount of mineral salts will vary according to the ph value of the water and the precise quantity of soda water that is mixed with the flour will depend on the atmospheric conditions. If it's damp after rain, or especially humid, less soda water should be used.

As Shohei tells Tampopo, to make ramen by hand requires great expertise. It is a great deal easier to buy an automatic noodle-making machine from Japan, which does all the work of kneading, resting, rolling and cutting the noodles for you. All the operator of such a machine has to do is ensure the quality of the flour in the hopper is good and starchy and that the computer controls are correctly set to mix no more than 2% water with the flour. Then he or she simply presses a button and a perfect portion of ramen rolls off the conveyor belt at the bottom of the machine.

Of course these machines are phenomenally expensive and there is absolutely no reason why anyone should invest in one, unless they are planning to open a noodle bar of their own. Noodles are never better than when they are hand-made by a master craftsman, but making ramen by hand is extremely difficult for an amateur. If you do want to make your own noodles at home, on the facing page you will find instructions for making menrui, the more traditional types of Japanese noodles, te'uchi (by hand).

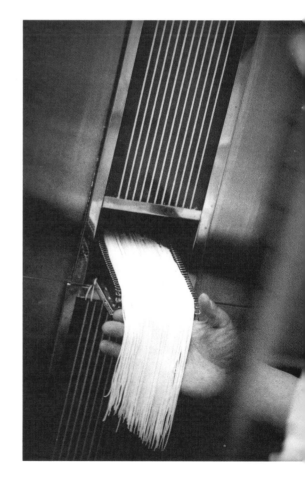

te'uchi (handmade) noodles

Making noodles by hand might seem a daunting process but, with practise, once each step has been mastered it is straightforward, enjoyable and surprisingly quick. The crucial point to bear in mind when making traditional Japanese noodles, which contain no egg to bind them, is that you must activate the natural gluten in the flour.

★ When using buckwheat flour, it is particularly important to knead the dough vigorously, to force the flour to yield up its sweetness. The recipe below can be adapted and the same procedures followed to make either udon or soba noodles, but udon are undeniably easier.

★ When you start to experiment with soba noodles, start by using only 4 parts buckwheat to 6 parts wheatflour. As you get the hang of it, you can gradually increase the proportion of buckwheat to 8 parts buckwheat to 2 parts wheatflour.

★ Another tip to increase the binding power of the flour is to use warm water (5–10 deg.C) in the first stages of mixing the dough. The warm water will encourage the starch in the flour to develop viscosity, making the dough more workable. You might also experiment by using Japanese green tea instead of plain water, which adds delicate nuances of colour and flavour to the finished noodles.

★ The addition of salt to the flour is vital, but exactly how much flour will depend on the hardness or softness of the water you are using.

★ It is important to rest the dough before rolling it, but for exactly how long will vary with the weather.

★ It is best to use the largest bowl you have to mix the flour and you will need a clean, dry work surface to roll out the dough. A master uses a rolling pin as long and thin as a broom handle, but any domestic rolling pin will suffice.

★ The only other equipment you will need is a roll of cling film to wrap the dough and a big knife to cut the noodles.

As you can see, there are variables for which the master noodle-maker develops an instinctive feel, but which even the beginner must bear in mind. A noodle master will even check the ph value of the water he is using every day before beginning to make noodles, and adjust his recipe accordingly. (Water for udon and soba should be as close to ph 7 – neutral – as possible.)

The neophyte cannot hope to get it right first time, or even the tenth time. However, as long as you make sure the flour you are using is fresh and well-sifted, and you learn the knack of mixing the water into the flour so that the dough develops its own elasticity, then you are half way to making a decent noodle.

ingredients

500g flour
200ml water, approximately
1 tablespoon of salt

method

★ Dissolve the salt in the water (it should be about as salty as seawater) and sift the flour into a bowl.

★ Make a well in the centre of the flour and slowly pour in three-quarters of the the water, mixing it in a circular motion with the fingers of your other hand. Avoid forming any large clumps of flour.

★ Using both hands, mix the moistened and dry flour together, squeezing it in your palms and allowing it to fall back into the bowl through your fingers. Continue for a few minutes, until the flour has absorbed all the water and started to form small pebbles.

★ Add the rest of the water to the pebbles of flour and continue mixing and squeezing until it is completely assimilated, then pack the dough together in the bowl.

★ Knead the dough in the bowl with a pumping action, utilising the strength of your whole arm by pressing down from the shoulder into the heel of your hand. Work the dough with one hand and, with the other, rotate the bowl every so often so that all the dough is thoroughly kneaded.

★ Continue to knead the dough until it is uniformly smooth and soft, but firm. The Japanese compare the texture of well-made noodle dough to the lobe of your ear. When you judge the dough to have reached that consistency, wrap it in cling film and set aside to rest.

★ If you are working in a centrally-heated kitchen, where it is warm, the dough will need to sit for only a couple of hours; if it is cold, then it would be better to leave it overnight. When you are ready to roll out the noodles, unwrap the dough from the cling film and divide into four smaller lumps of equal size and put them into a bowl, covering with a damp cloth to prevent them from drying out.

★ Sprinkle some plain flour over the surface you are intending to work on to stop the dough from sticking. Take one lump at a time, roll it between your palms to make a ball, then place it on the work surface and flatten it slightly with your palm.

★ With the rolling pin, roll out the dough in a shape that is as rectangular as possible, to a thickness of a couple of centimetres.

★ Set the rolled-out sheet of dough to one side and sprinkle its surface with flour. Repeat steps eight and nine, rolling out the other lumps of dough, and stack the sheets on top of each other with a sprinkling of flour between them to stop them from sticking.

★ Cut the stacked sheets of dough in half and fold each half in half again, with the cut ends neatly aligned.

★ Working from the cut, straight edge, slice the dough into strips with a large knife, moving it firmly and smoothly through the dough.

★ Shake out the noodles, separating the strands. If kept refridgerated in a plastic bag they will last for up to a week.

'noodles are synergistic things. every step must be perfectly built. don't forget that.'

THE MASTER, *TAMPOPO*

'Today,' declares Goro, 'we start making *Lai Lai* a "three star" noodle joint. Master, you handle the soup. Shohei, starting today, you're responsible for the noodles. Gun and myself, we will take charge of the atmosphere. We will create rich depth and a clear, shoyu-flavoured soup. We'll add only shinachiku roots and spring onions. The menu will offer only plain noodles and pork noodles. Agreed?'

The partners do agree, although the menu is later extended when Pisken joins the team and introduces his Spring Onion Special. Pisken is a drunken loudmouth, with whom Goro had a fight back at the beginning of the movie, but he turned out to be not such a bad guy. A building contractor, specialising in casino interiors, he offers to renovate the grimy premises of *Lai Lai* into a temple of simple gastronomic pleasure.

The Master proposes that since the noodles will change, the name of the noodle shop should change too. They need a name that is different, easy to say, feminine too, and taste-tempting. Goro thinks of the perfect name: '*Tampopo*!'

The widow Tampopo takes the enigmatic trucker out to dinner to get to know him better and to thank him for helping her. 'It's like we all have our own ladder,' she tells him. 'Some climb the rungs to the top, but some don't even know they have one. You helped me find my ladder.'

Having found her ladder and become fully committed to the Way of the Noodle, Tampopo perseveres in her quest for perfection...

Goro, Gun, Shohei, the Master and Pisken are her critics. They sit like a jury along the counter of the shop to sample her noodles. 'They are beginning to have depth,' is the verdict, 'but they still lack substance. They are not alive enough. They lack vigour and they still lack profundity.'

Tampopo is not deterred by this honest criticism, but continues to apply herself. Eventually, but inevitably, the day dawns when, one by one, the members of the jury drain their bowls to the last drop. At last, Goro can say to his diligent student, 'Congratulations! You've done it!'

wagapopo

Like Tampopo, we at wagamama are diligent students of the Way of the Noodle. We, too, aspire to ascend the ladder of ramenology. When one has learned to cook ramen, to make soup, to prepare the toppings and to assemble a noodle soup with good grace, however, there is yet one rung to climb. For a dish to be completely satisfactory, it must not only smell divine and taste delicious, but first and foremost it must look delightful.

The arrangement of the toppings on a bowl of ramen is an art comparable to ikebana, the Japanese art of flower arranging, or to calligraphy. The form is critical. The dish should look inviting, of course, but to be wholly appealing a bowl of ramen must also appear beautifully balanced and harmonious. In this way, the presentation of food is a reminder of the underlying principle of yin and yang.

To give the ramen room to breathe and the ramenologist a good-sized canvas on which to work, it is best to serve noodle soups in big bowls. A common Japanese simile likens the food on a plate to mountains, the spaces between each morsel are valleys. Similarly, when composing noodle soups, be aware of the spatial relationships between ingredients. Should the chicken slices go on the right or left side of the bowl? Should the beansprouts be sprinkled all over the surface or arranged in the middle? Where would this sprig of coriander look best? There are no hard answers to these questions, but with practice and the correct attitude of humility, the ardent noodle cook should quickly develop a feel for the way these things should be.

how to boil water

★ The most crucial stage, which appears in all the recipes, is the boiling of the noodles.

★ How much cooking your noodles will require depends upon how fresh they are. If you are using freshly-made noodles, they will need to be immersed in boiling water for only a couple of minutes. If the noodles are dried, they will need to be cooked for longer, perhaps 10–15 minutes.

★ The noodles must be cooked through, but still be quite firm and slightly chewy (what the Italians call 'al dente'). The noodles for a soup dish should even be slightly undercooked, since they will finish cooking in the hot broth that is poured over them.

★ It is essential that you boil noodles in plenty of water, so that they are not so tightly crowded that they stick together and there is plenty of room for the water to circulate around them. The correct ratio of noodles to water are: for ramen, 1:10; for soba noodles, 1:20. When cooking noodles, remember that there is no such thing as too much water and use the largest pot that you have available. There is no need to add salt.

★ To cook the noodles, bring a large pot of water to a full, rolling boil. Add the noodles gradually to the boiling water, so as not to reduce its temperature too quickly. If you are using fresh noodles, simply turn down the heat under the pan once the water has come back to a full boil and simmer for only a minute or so, stirring carefully so as not to break the noodles. Check that the noodles are cooked by biting into one, or by throwing it at the wall. If it sticks, the noodle is cooked.

★ If you are using dried noodles, the 'shock' method is a better way to boil them. As the noodles start to cook, their starch begins to dissolve and a white foam will rapidly form on the surface of the boiling water. As this foam boils up the sides of the pan, add a cup of cold water to reduce the temperature. Repeat this procedure when the water comes back to the boil. When the water boils for a third time, check to see if the noodles are cooked. If not, add another cup of cold water and boil once more until they are cooked.

★ When the noodles are cooked, remove them using a long-handled sieve, or strain them into a colander, and rinse them under cold running water. This will stop the cooking process (which will be completed when you pour the hot soup over them) and wash off excess starch.

★ The noodles can be reheated before use by briefly plunging them, still in the sieve or colander, into boiling water. Separate out the strands by shaking the sieve.

NB: Before attempting any of the recipes, refer to page 91.

chicken ramen

In this dish, our customers' all-time favourite, the chicken is marinaded in teriyaki sauce before being seared on a grill, or in a heavy-bottomed frying pan, sliced and served on top of the ramen with bright green steamed spinach leaves and fresh beansprouts, menma and spring onions.

Commercially-bottled teriyaki sauce is an acceptable alternative to making your own, but it is easily prepared if you have the ingredients. The proportions given below can be used to make any quantity of sauce, which can be kept indefinitely as long as it is in a sealed bottle in the fridge.

ingredients

125g ramen noodles
350ml basic ramen soup stock

for the teriyaki sauce:
7 teaspoons dark soy sauce
7 teaspoons sake
7 teaspoons mirin
1 teaspoon sugar

for the topping:
1 chicken breast
4 fresh spinach leaves, or other seasonal greens
2 spring onions, finely chopped
6 pieces menma

to garnish:
1 spring onion, finely chopped

method

★ Combine the teriyaki sauce ingredients in a bowl, then coat the chicken breast with the mixture and leave to marinate for at least an hour.

★ Grill the chicken breast for five to ten minutes until it is cooked through and firm to the touch, brushing frequently with the teriyaki sauce to glaze it while cooking.

★ Steam the spinach.

★ Heat the soup stock and boil the noodles.

★ Arrange the cooked noodles in the bowl. Slice the chicken and arrange the pieces on top of the noodles, with the spinach and menma.

★ Carefully pour the hot chicken soup stock over the noodles to cover them and garnish with chopped spring onion.

chilli beef ramen

The powerful flavour of chargrilled steak and onion is complemented by fiery green chillis and cooled by coriander and mint in this pungent and warming ramen dish. For extra flavour, marinate the steak in teriyaki sauce for an hour before use and prepare some onion by finely chopping, then deep frying a couple of shallots and drain them well.

The soup is flavoured with chilli sauce, mixed with Oriental fish sauce (sold under various brand names in Oriental supermarkets), soy sauce and vinegar. The dish is served with a separate dish of beansprouts, coriander and a wedge of lime. To further enhance the flavour and provide contrasting texture, squirt the lime into the soup and sprinkle the beansprouts and coriander on top.

ingredients

125g ramen noodles
350ml basic ramen soup stock

for the chilli base:
1 tablespoon chilli sauce
1 teaspoon fish sauce
$1/2$ teaspoon dark soy sauce
1 teaspoon rice vinegar
1 teaspoon mirin

for the topping:
120–130g prime rump steak marinated in teriyaki sauce (see page 34)
2 red chillis, sliced lengthways, deseeded and finely sliced
$1/4$ onion, thinly sliced
1 spring onion, finely chopped
a sprig of mint

to garnish:
30g (or a handful) beansprouts, topped and tailed
30g (or a handful) coriander leaves, washed and carefully picked
finely chopped, deep-fried shallots
1 wedge of lime

method

★ Sear the marinated steak on a hot grill or frying pan and cook for three to four minutes each side, until the meat becomes firm when you prod it. When it is nearly cooked, remove from the grill briefly and coat with teriyaki sauce before returning to the grill to finish cooking.

★ Boil the noodles.

★ Mix the chilli base ingredients and heat the soup stock, adding the chilli base to taste.

★ Arrange the noodles in the bowl and pour the soup over them. Slice the steak and arrange the pieces on top of the noodles. Garnish with the shredded green chilli and sprinkle deep-fried shallots over the whole bowl.

★ Serve with a separate bowl of beansprouts and coriander, plus a wedge of lime.

wagamama ramen

For wagamama ramen, we prefer to use the same
teriyaki chicken as we do for the chicken ramen.
You might use any cooked chicken that you happen
to have, or a raw breast, which can be shredded
and steamed along with the other toppings.

ingredients

125g ramen noodles
350ml basic ramen soup stock

for the toppings:
$1/2$ a boiled egg
4 fresh spinach leaves, or other seasonal greens
1 slice naruto fishcake
1 prawn
2 slices cooked teriyaki chicken
1 crabstick
1 cube deep-fried tofu
6 pieces menma
a few pieces reconstituted wakame

to garnish:
1 spring onion, finely chopped

method

★ Boil the egg for five minutes, then put it into cold
water. After ten minutes, peel and cut the egg in
half.

★ Lightly steam the prawn and spinach and the
chicken, too, if necessary.

★ Boil the noodles and heat the soup.

★ Arrange the noodles in the bowl, pour the stock
over them and place the steamed prawn and
spinach, the chicken and crabstick, with the tofu,
menma, naruto and wakame on top. Add the
garnish and serve.

char su ramen

This classic ramen dish with slices of roast pork, as seen in *Tampopo,* is very Chinese. The char su pork is marinaded with hoi sin barbecue sauce and the soup is enlivened with five spice powder, a fiery condiment available from Oriental supermarkets. Char su ramen is conventionally served in a thick pork soup stock, with jewels of fat glinting on the surface. At wagamama, we prefer a lighter and less fatty, chicken-based soup stock.

ingredients

125g cooked ramen noodles
350ml basic ramen soup stock

for the pork marinade:
$1/2$ teaspoon salt
2 tablespoons sugar
1 tablespoon beaten egg
1 teaspoon hoi sin barbecue sauce
$1/2$ tablespoon sake
1 tablespoon light soy sauce
1 large pinch five spice powder

for the topping:
150—200g lean pork
4 fresh spinach leaves or other seasonal greens
6 pieces menma

method

★ Mix the marinade ingredients and marinate the pork for at least an hour before roasting it in the oven for about 20 minutes, until it is cooked.

★ Steam the spinach.

★ Boil the noodles and heat the soup.

★ Arrange the cooked noodles in the bowl, pour the soup over them and arrange the pork slices with the spinach on top. Serve.

chuka ramen

Another overtly Chinese-influenced dish -- 'chuka' means Chinese – this is basically a seafood stir-fry thickened with cornflour and served with a meaty stock and garnished with wood ear fungus, which is available in dried form from Oriental supermarkets and must be reconstituted with water before use.

ingredients

125g ramen noodles
350ml basic ramen soup stock

for the topping:
1/2 courgette, sliced diagonally 3mm thick
2 pieces wood ear fungus
8 prawns, shelled and de-veined
2 shiitake mushrooms, sliced
30g (or a small handful) thinly-sliced leek
1 quail's egg
1 clove crushed garlic

to season and thicken the stir-fry:
2 teaspoons light soy sauce
1 teaspoon mirin
100ml stock or water
1/2 teaspoon cornflour with 2 teaspoons water

to coat the prawns:
1 egg white
sesame oil
salt and pepper
cornflour for dredging the prawns

method

★ Poach the quail's egg for five minutes in boiling water, then leave it to stand in cold water until needed.

★ Mix the prawns with a pinch of salt and pepper, a few drops of sesame oil, a tablespoon of egg white and a teaspoon of cornflour. Ensure the prawns are throughly coated in this mixture, then quickly fry them in a little cooking oil for a couple of minutes, and drain them onto a plate.

★ Put the crushed garlic into a frying pan or wok with a teaspoon of oil and cook until it starts to turn brown. Then add the courgette, shiitake, shredded leek and wood ear fungus and stir-fry for three to five minutes, turning the vegetables continuously. Next add 100ml stock or water. Then add the prawns.

★ Season the stir-fry with a large pinch of salt, a teaspoon of mirin, and two teaspoons of light soy sauce and finish by adding the cornflour mixture to thicken it.

★ Boil the noodles and heat the soup stock.

★ Arrange the cooked noodles in a bowl, pour the soup over them, and arrange the stir-fry on top. Peel the boiled quail's egg and place it in the centre of the bowl.

salmon ramen

Farmed salmon is relatively cheap these days, although some people will tell you that it doesn't have much flavour. When brushed with teriyaki sauce whilst grilling, and served in a bowl of aromatic fishy soup, however, it can be sensational. The latest wagamama improvement to this recipe is to add minced shallots and ginger, which have been cooked until crispy and flavoured with shoyu. Try it!

ingredients

125g ramen noodles
350ml fish soup stock

for the topping:
1 slice salmon fillet, 3—4cm thick
4 leaves of spinach or other seasonal greens
6 pieces menma
teriyaki sauce (see page 34)

to garnish:
1 piece ginger, about the size of your thumb, peeled and finely chopped
2 shallots, finely chopped
1 spring onion, finely chopped
1 or 2 cloves minced garlic
soy sauce

method

★ Put the minced ginger and garlic into a frying pan with a drop of cooking oil and cook for a few minutes, until the mixture turns golden brown and starts to smell quite strong. Add a teaspoonful of light soy sauce, remove from the heat and put to one side.

★ Grill the salmon, brushing with teriyaki sauce to glaze it as it cooks.

★ Steam the spinach.

★ Boil the noodles and heat the soup.

★ Arrange the cooked noodles in the bowl, pour the fish stock over them and put the cooked salmon with the greens and menma on top. Sprinkle the fried ginger and shallots over the assembled dish and garnish with chopped spring onion.

seafood ramen

Fresh, lightly-steamed seafood, including prawns and squid, a scallop and a crabstick are combined in this simple ramen dish. If you cannot get fresh squid, frozen will do.

ingredients

125g ramen noodles
350ml fish soup stock

for the topping:
2 prawns
3 slices of squid, about 6cm long
1 scallop
1 crabstick
1 slice naruto
4 spinach leaves or other seasonal greens
6 pieces of menma

to garnish:
a few pieces reconstituted wakame
2 spring onions, finely chopped

method

★ Steam the prawns, squid, scallop and spinach for a couple of minutes, without overcooking them.

★ Boil the noodles and heat the fish soup stock.

★ Arrange the noodles in the bowl, pour the soup stock over them and arrange the toppings. Garnish with wakame and chopped spring onions. Serve.

moyashi soba

Historically misnamed soba, because it tastes so wholesome, this healthy vegetarian dish is strictly vegan. It consists of stir-fried courgette, mange touts, leek, mushrooms and beansprouts, with some deep-fried tofu thrown in for added protein and garlic for extra flavour. Tofu is sold in standard-sized blocks, which is enough for two portions. Cut the block of tofu in half, then divide half the block into quarters. Deep-fry the four cubes of tofu in soya oil.

Delicate enoki mushrooms are well suited to moyashi soba and can be found, vacuum-packed, in grocery stores. Use them raw.

ingredients

125g ramen noodles
350ml vegetarian soup stock

for the topping:
1/2 courgette
1/2 smallish leek
some mange touts, topped and tailed
a handful beansprouts
a few sliced button mushrooms
slivers dried garlic, to taste
4 cubes deep-fried tofu

to season and thicken the stir-fry:
light soy sauce
sesame oil
salt and pepper
100ml water or stock
1/2 teaspoon cornflour mixed with 2 teaspoons water

to garnish:
some enoki mushrooms
1 spring onion, finely chopped

method

★ Wash and prepare the vegetables to be stir-fried by cutting them into strips approximately 6cm long by 1cm wide.

★ Stir-fry the cut vegetables for a couple of minutes, until cooked but still crisp, then add a ladle (about half a cup) of cold water or vegetable stock, and season with salt and pepper, a few drops of sesame oil and a dash of light soy sauce. Finally, thicken with the cornflour mixture.

★ Heat and season the vegetarian soup and boil water for noodles.

★ Stir fry the vegetables in a little soya oil.

★ Cook the noodles and place in a bowl. Pour the broth over the noodles and arrange the stir-fried vegetables on top. Garnish with fresh enoki mushrooms. Serve immediately.

miso ramen

A hearty, healthy ramen dish at any time of the year, miso ramen is especially popular during the winter months. This version is pepped up with garlic purée, which can be bought in tubes from supermarkets, although it is easy to make your own by whizzing fresh garlic in a blender with some olive oil.

ingredients

125g ramen noodles
350ml basic ramen soup stock

for the miso soup base:
1 tablespoon miso paste
$1/2$ teaspoon sesame oil
$1/2$ teaspoon garlic purée
1 teaspoon mirin
small pinch of chilli powder
pinch of white pepper
pinch of salt, to taste

for the topping:
100g cooked shredded chicken
$1/2$ large carrot
$1/2$ medium-sized leek
50g (a large handful) beansprouts
6 pieces menma
some pieces of reconstituted wakame
1 shiitake mushroom
1 pinch sesame seeds

to season the stir-fry:
white pepper and salt to taste
2 teaspoons light soy sauce
1 teaspoon mirin
sesame oil

to coat the chicken:
2 teaspoons cornflour
$1/2$ teaspoon light soy sauce
1 teaspoon mirin
the white of an egg, beaten
a few drops of sesame oil
$1/2$ teaspoon cornflour with 2 teaspoons water

method

★ Prepare the vegetables for stir-frying by washing and cutting the carrot and leek into strips approximately 6cm long and 1cm wide; remove the stalk from the shiitake and slice it.

★ Stir-fry the shredded chicken with the carrot, leek and shiitake for three to five minutes. Finish by seasoning with a large pinch of salt, white pepper, soy sauce and mirin.

★ Boil the noodles and heat the soup. Add the miso base and stir thoroughly to ensure it dissolves.

★ Arrange the noodles in the bowl and pour the miso soup over them. Arrange the stir-fry on top, garnish with wakame and sprinkle with sesame seeds and a few drops of sesame oil before serving.

zazai ramen'

Not unlike chilli chicken ramen, zazai is enlivened
with chilli paste and crunchy preserved mustard
vegetables, which are popular throughout the East.
Mustard greens, also known as Chinese radish, are
canned, whole or shredded, in various regions and
sold under many different brand names. Ask in your
local Oriental supermarket which types they have
available.

Commercially bottled chilli sauce is an acceptable
alternative to making your own; otherwise take a
teaspoon each of minced ginger and garlic, a couple
of diced shallots and half a teaspoon (or a few
generous pinches) each of red pepper, salt, sugar
and chilli powder. Put the lot into a food processor
and whizz it up, adding vegetable oil until it forms a
paste. Scrape the paste into a pan, add two
tablespoons of vegetable oil and cook over medium
heat, stirring frequently, for half an hour. If the
mixture sticks, or begins to burn, add some more
oil and turn down the heat.

ingredients

125g ramen noodles
350ml basic ramen soup stock

for the topping:
100g shredded chicken
3 shiitake mushrooms
1 spring onion, cut at an angle into 3—4cm strips
40g or a heaped tablespoon of preserved
mustard vegetables
a dollop of chilli sauce

to season and thicken the stir-fry:
mirin
light soy sauce
sesame oil
salt and pepper

100ml water or stock
$1/2$ teaspoon of cornflour mixed with 2 teaspoons
water

to coat the chicken:
2 teaspoons cornflour
$1/2$ teaspoon light soy sauce
1 teaspoon mirin
the white of an egg, beaten
a few drops of sesame oil
$1/2$ teaspoon cornflour with 2 teaspoons water

method

★ Combine the ingredients for coating the chicken,
adding the beaten egg white last. The mixture must
be thick enough to coat the chicken, so add only
enough egg white to achieve a workable
consistency. Then coat the shredded chicken in the
cornflour mixture and fry it over a medium heat for
a few minutes, until the chicken is nearly cooked –
its colour should have just started to change.

★ Stir-fry the shiitake mushrooms, chicken and
preserved vegetables for three to five minutes,
then add the spring onion. Finish the stir-fry by
pouring in 100ml of water, or stock, season with
soy and mirin, and thicken with the cornflour
mixture.

★ Boil the noodles and heat the soup.

★ Arrange the noodles in the bowl, pour the soup
over them and arrange the stir-fry on top. Garnish
with a dollop of chilli sauce before serving.

kake soba

The most ordinary way to enjoy Japanese noodles is in a bowl of hot, shoyu-flavoured dashi broth, garnished with finely-chopped spring onions. This is the most elementary noodle soup recipe. It can be made using either soba or udon and should be used as a basis for experimentation.

The simplicity of kake soba does not mean that it is easy to get right the first time you try to make it, but the first time you make it you will not know how it should taste. The flavour is largely dependent on the flavour base of soy sauce and mirin that you add to the dashi broth. For added flavour, try adding some grated ginger or, if you have a juice extractor, fresh ginger juice is dynamite!

ingredients

125g soba noodles
350ml dashi broth

for the topping:
1 teaspoon finely chopped or grated ginger
1 teaspoon finely shredded nori
2 chopped spring onions

method

★ Heat the dashi, adding the soy sauce and mirin flavour base and the grated ginger. Taste the broth and add more soy, or mirin, to adjust the taste if necessary.

★ Boil the noodles.

★ Assemble the dish by arranging the cooked noodles in a bowl and pouring the broth over them.

★ Garnish the dish by sprinkling the chopped spring onions and shredded nori over the surface and serve immediately.

tempura soba

One of the most popular dishes at the swankiest soba shops in Tokyo, there are several permutations of tempura soba. Scallops may be used instead of king prawns, and the tempura may be served sizzling in the soup, or as a side dish, so that the batter retains its crispness.

Making tempura is not as difficult as it might seem, as long as you bear in mind three vital points: the ingredients must be fresh enough to eat raw; the oil must be at a constant temperature; the batter must be slightly lumpy, not smooth. Make the batter for immediate use, while the oil is getting hot, and do not mix it too thoroughly.

Remember that you are not making pancakes, but trying to produce a light and lacy, crisp and golden coating for the king prawns. It is important that the water you use is ice cold and the batter is never left to stand for longer than a few minutes.

ingredients

125g soba noodles
350ml dashi broth

for the topping:
2 king prawns
sifted cornflour to dredge the prawns
1 tablespoon shredded nori

for the tempura batter:
2 egg yolks
200ml cold water
100g flour

method

★ Combine the egg yolk with the cold water in a bowl, whisking with a fork or a pair of chopsticks. Sift the flour and gently stir into the mixture using a figure of eight motion.

★ Heat the dashi broth and boil water for the noodles.

★ Heat a pan or wok full of vegetable oil to deep-fry the tempura. You can check the temperature by dripping a dollop of batter into the oil. If it sinks the oil is too cold; if it skids across the surface the oil is too hot. It has reached the right temperature, (170°C,) when the batter sinks slightly and bobs immediately back to the surface.

★ Clean, de-vein, wash and pat dry the king prawns with a paper towel. This is essential for the batter to adhere properly. Score the undersides of the prawns with a knife, so they don't curl up too much when cooked.

★ Dredge the prawns in the sifted cornflour before dipping them into the batter and then into the hot oil. Cook each piece until it is yellow rather than golden and crisp on the outside.

★ Boil the noodles and, when they're cooked, arrange them in a bowl and pour the soup over them. As soon as the tempura is ready, arrange it on top of the noodles, garnish with the shredded nori, and serve immediately.

tori nanba soba

In Osaka, this dish is made using udon noodles and the green onions that were once grown in the Nanba district of the city. This adaptation uses leek, which has a similarly mild flavour, and soba noodles. The chicken is cooked 'Chinese style': that is to say, dredged in cornflour and deep fried.

ingredients

125g soba noodles
350ml dashi broth

for the topping:
1 chicken breast
1 egg white
2 tablespoons cornflour
salt and pepper
1 leek

for the garnish:
3 slices kamaboko fishcake
1 teaspoon of shredded nori

method

★ Heat a pan of soya oil in which to deep-fry the chicken. Season the flour with salt and pepper. Lightly beat the egg white with a fork and use it to lightly coat the chicken breast, which is then dredged in the seasoned cornflour. Deep-fry the chicken in the hot oil until the flour coating is crisp and golden.

★ Slice the leek lengthways, wash it under cold running water, then slice into long, thin strips. Stir-fry the leek in a little sesame oil over high heat for half a minute, then add the soy sauce and mirin and cook for a further thirty seconds.

★ Boil the noodles; drain, and arrange them in the bowl.

★ Slice the chicken into thin, bite-sized pieces and arrange them with the cooked leek on top of the noodles, then pour the broth over the other ingredients. Garnish with the sliced kamaboko and shredded nori, and serve immediately.

kitsune udon

The wily fox (kitsune), in Japanese folklore, is particularly partial to a tofu preparation called aburage. Thin sheets of tofu cake which have been deep-fried, aburage is usually sold, refridgerated, in packets of three or five. Mr Fox would certainly be tempted by this dish, in which the light and absorbent tofu becomes juicy and chewy when saturated with delicious dashi broth.

ingredients

125g udon noodles
350ml dashi broth

for the topping:
1 sheet aburage
2 spring onions, finely chopped
some shredded nori

for the simmering stock:
200ml dashi 2
30ml or 2 tablespoons soy sauce
15ml or 1 tablespoon mirin

method

★ Pour boiling water over the aburage to remove excess oil, and drain it thoroughly.

★ Combine the simmering stock ingredients in a small saucepan and heat to boiling point. When the mixture begins to foam, put in the washed aburage, put a lid on the saucepan and turn down the heat to simmer. Continue to simmer for about ten minutes, or until the stock is absorbed, turning the aburage at least once.

★ While the aburage simmers, heat the broth and boil the noodles.

★ Put the noodles into the bowl and arrange the cooked aburage on top of them. Pour the dashi broth over the aburage and noodles. Garnish with chopped spring onion and shredded nori. Serve immediately.

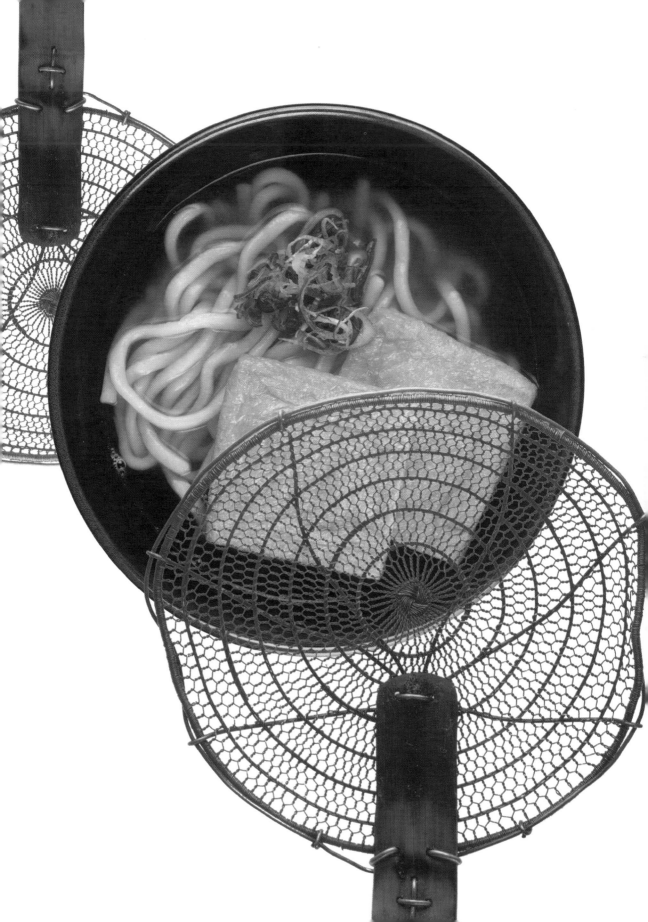

tsukimi udon

'Tsukimi' means 'moon-viewing'. Admiring the moon is a traditional autumnal activity in the south of Japan, where udon noodles are most popular. In this dish, a raw egg is lightly poached in the hot broth, giving the yolk a slightly misty surface, like a perfect full moon among clouds of udon.

Kamaboko (or naruto) fish cake is a nice accompaniment, but not necessary to the spirit of tsukimi udon. What is important in this dish is the egg; try to find one that has been freshly laid by a free range chicken!

ingredients

125g udon noodles
350ml dashi broth

for the topping:
1 fresh egg
3 slices kamaboko fish cake
1 small sheet nori, cut into strips
2 spring onions, finely chopped

method

★ Heat the dashi broth and boil the noodles.

★ Arrange the noodles around the sides of the bowl to make a nest in the middle for the eggy moon. Arrange the kamaboko at one side.

★ Carefully pour in the dashi broth, which must be very hot, until the noodles are just covered. With the back of a large spoon or ladle, reinforce the nest in the middle of the noodles.

★ Crack an egg, taking care not to break the yolk, and pour it into the noodle nest. Cover the bowl with a plate for a minute before serving, to let the egg yolk become slightly poached.

★ Garnish with the shredded nori and spring onion. Serve immediately.

nabeyaki udon

A hearty noodle stew for a cold day, nabeyaki is like a baby sukiyaki, individually served in small earthenware casseroles. Like tsukimi udon, nabeyaki contains a raw egg that is lightly poached in the dashi broth, so that when it is broken with the tips of the chopsticks, the yolk mixes with the broth and slightly thickens it.

This version of the nabeyaki casserole uses chicken, complimented by the subtle flavour of shiitake mushrooms, but any number of ingredients can be added or substituted. Why not try this method using a light vegetarian dashi, scallops and chrysanthemum leaves? It might be even nicer served with prawn tempura!

ingredients

125g udon noodles
350ml dashi broth

for the topping:
1 chicken breast
4 or 5 peeled prawns
2 large shiitake mushrooms
wakame seaweed, according to taste
3 slices kamaboko fish cake
2 spring onions, finely chopped
30g (or a handful) bamboo shoots
1 fresh egg.

for the simmering stock:
200ml dashi 2
30ml or 2 tablespoons soy sauce
15ml or 1 tablespoon mirin

method

★ Remove the stems from the shiitake mushrooms and cut a cross in their caps.

★ Cut the chicken into bite-sized strips and briefly stir-fry them, and the prawns, in a little sesame oil.

★ Add the shiitake caps to the wok (or frying pan) and pour in the simmering stock ingredients. When it begins to boil, turn down the heat, put a lid on the pan, and simmer for 15 minutes.

★ While the other ingredients simmer, heat the dashi broth and boil the noodles. Put the cooked noodles into the casserole and, when the simmered chicken, prawns and mushrooms are cooked, arrange them on top of the noodles and pour the hot broth over, to fill the casserole almost to its brim.

★ Put the lid on the casserole and slowly bring the contents to the boil, using moderate heat. When the broth begins to bubble up under the lid, remove it, turn down the heat and skim any scum from the surface with a spoon.

★ With the back of a large spoon or ladle, make an indentation in the noodles, a nest into which you can put the egg. Crack the egg, being careful not to break the yolk, and pour it into the nest you have made. Count to 101 to allow the egg to cook before serving.

kare udon

The Japanese adore the flavour of curry, which goes particularly well with fat udon. The curry sauce we prefer at wagamama has a Thai accent, made with red curry paste (available from Oriental supermarkets) and finished with coconut milk. As this is not a soup-based dish, increase the quantity of noodles to 200g for a substantial portion.

ingredients

200g udon noodles

for the curry paste:
2 cloves of garlic
2 shallots
peeled ginger, about the size of your thumb
1 dessertspoon curry powder
1 dessertspoon Thai red curry paste
2 dessertspoons tomato ketchup
150ml ($1/2$ can) coconut milk

for the topping:
4 prawns
4 pieces squid, about 6cm long
5 cubes deep-fried tofu
30g (or a handful) French green beans, cut in half

for seasoning:
1 teaspoon mirin

for garnish:
coriander

method

★ Whizz the garlic, shallots and ginger in a blender or food processor.

★ Heat a couple of teaspoons of vegetable oil in a frying pan or wok, add the blended ingredients and cook for a few minutes over medium heat before adding the curry powder, ketchup and French beans.

★ Add the squid, prawns and tofu to the curry mixture and cook them for a few minutes. Then add the coconut milk. Remove from heat, check the flavour and add mirin to season.

★ Boil the noodles.

★ Arrange the bowls on a large, shallow plate and pour the curried mixture over them.

★ Garnish with chopped coriander and serve.

pan-fried noodles

yaki soba

At wagamama, we have a large, cast iron griddle on which to prepare our pan-fried noodles. At home, use a heavy-bottomed frying pan or a heavy-duty wok. If possible, cook over a gas ring burner rather than electricity, as it is appreciably hotter. For yaki soba — which is traditionally made with ramen noodles, not proper soba noodles — we use special flat noodles, a bit like linguine, which take the heat better. You can use standard ramen noodles.

Lightly-salted pickled ginger is red in colour and shredded rather than sliced, like sushi ginger. It is good with yaki soba and can be bought from Oriental supermarkets.

ingredients

200g cooked ramen noodles

for the topping:
1/2 onion, thinly sliced
30g (or a handful) shredded carrots
100g beansprouts
30g (or a handful) thinly-sliced green pepper
50g shredded cooked chicken
6 cooked shrimps
1 egg

for seasoning:
1 dessertspoon light soy sauce
1/2 teaspoon salt
1 teaspoon mirin
a few drops of sesame oil

to garnish:
pickled ginger
sesame seeds
1 spring onion, finely chopped

method

★ Put all the ingredients, except the egg, into a bowl with the seasoning and mix them with your hand. Then crack the egg into the bowl and mix it thoroughly.

★ Heat a couple of teaspoons of vegetable oil in a wok or frying pan until the oil starts to smoke.

★ Put the mixed ingredients into the hot pan and fry until golden, stirring occasionally with a wooden spoon.

★ Turn the cooked noodles onto a plate, garnish with pickled ginger, chopped spring onion and sprinkled sesame seeds.

yaki udon

Yaki chikura is a type of Japanese fishcake, like naruto and kamaboko, which is typically used in yaki udon. Do not try to substitute either of the other varieties of fishcake in this recipe, as they will disintegrate with the heat.

ingredients

200g cooked udon noodles

for the topping:
25g shredded leek
30g shredded cooked chicken
100g beansprouts
25g finely sliced red pepper
6 slices yaki chikura
6 sliced shiitake mushrooms
2 prawns, shelled and de-veined
1 egg

for seasoning:
1 dessertspoon light soy sauce
$1/2$ teaspoon salt
1 dessertspoon chilli oil
1 teaspoon mirin
a few drops sesame oil

to garnish:
Thai chilli powder with shrimps
pickles
1 spring onion, finely chopped

method

★ Put all the ingredients, except the egg, into a bowl with the seasoning and mix them with your hand. Then crack the egg into the bowl and mix it thoroughly.

★ Heat a couple of teaspoons of vegetable oil in a wok or frying pan until the oil starts to smoke.

★ Put the mixed ingredients into the hot pan and fry until golden, stirring occasionally with a wooden spoon.

★ Turn the cooked noodles onto a plate, garnish with pickles, some dried shrimps, a sprinkling of chilli powder, and chopped spring onion.

yasai yaki soba

A strictly vegetarian version of yaki soba, using buckwheat noodles, this is a power-packed noodle dish made tastier with the addition of the yasai sauce, which is poured over the cooked noodles just before serving.

ingredients

200g cooked soba noodles

for the topping:
30g shredded carrots
30g thinly-sliced green peppers
2 sliced shiitake mushrooms
1 egg

for seasoning:
1 dessertspoon light soy sauce
$1/2$ teaspoon salt
1 teaspoon mirin
a few drops sesame oil

for the yasai sauce:
1 dessertspoon mirin
$1/2$ dessertspoon rice vinegar
$1/2$ dessertspoon light soy sauce
a few drops sesame oil
1 teaspoon each of finely chopped green and red peppers, coriander and ginger

to garnish:
pickles
sesame seeds
1 spring onion, finely chopped

method

★ Put all the ingredients, except the egg, into a bowl with the seasoning and mix them with your hand. Then crack the egg into the bowl and mix it thoroughly.

★ Heat a couple of teaspoons of vegetable oil in a wok or frying pan until the oil starts to smoke.

★ Put the mixed ingredients into the hot pan and fry until golden, stirring occasionally with a wooden spoon.

★ Combine the ingredients of the yasai sauce and, taking it off the heat, mix it in with the cooked noodles. Then turn the noodles out onto a plate and garnish with pickles, finely chopped spring onion and a sprinkling of sesame seeds.

cold noodle dishes

zaru soba

Serving soba noodles in the nude, cold and unadorned save by the most ordinary garnishes, is the most daring dish in the soba master's repertoire. The lack of distracting flavours allows the connoisseur to savour the special sweetness of the buckwheat and to appreciate the silky texture of a true craftsman's noodles.

Because pure buckwheat noodles are delicate, they were frequently steamed rather than boiled. Zaru soba is still served in stylised steamer baskets, looking like square lacquered boxes with slatted bottoms, as a reminder of the traditional ways.

The noodles are accompanied by a cold, strong dipping sauce made from a base of dashi 2, flavoured with shoyu and mirin. This sauce can be made up to the proportions given below, adjusted according to taste, and kept in the fridge for up to two months. Serve it with a dollop of wasabi, the hot Japanese horseradish paste, on the side.

Even if you are not yet a master of te'uchi noodles, eager to show off your expertise, store-bought soba noodles can also make a refreshing meal for a hot day. If you have a plain bamboo steamer basket to serve them in, so much the better.

ingredients

125g soba noodles

for the dipping sauce:
125ml dashi 2
2–3 tablespoons soy sauce
1–2 tablespoons mirin
salt and sugar to taste

to garnish:
1–2 sheets of nori, shredded
30g grated daikon
2 spring onions, finely chopped
1 dollop wasabi

method

★ Combine the dipping sauce ingredients and refrigerate.

★ Cook the noodles according to the shock method (see page 33) and plunge the cooked noodles into iced water.

★ Drain the cold noodles thoroughly, arrange them in the basket and sprinkle the shredded nori over them. Serve the grated daikon, chopped spring onion and the dipping sauce in separate bowls. Add the chopped spring onion and wasabi to the sauce to taste.

spicy soba salad

A healthy pasta salad made with soba noodles and steamed vegetables, dressed with a sesame oil dressing spiked with chilli. To make the noodles easier to mix with the vegetables, break them into pieces 10–12 cm long before cooking.

ingredients

125g soba noodles

for the topping:
carrots, cut into strips 6cm by 1cm
broccoli florets
green peppers, de-seeded and cut into strips
mange touts topped and tailed
fresh coriander, chopped

for the dressing:
1 dessertspoon rice vinegar
1 dessertspoon light soy sauce
2 dessertspoons mirin
1 dessertspoon tahini
$1/2$ dessertspoon sake
1 dessertspoon sesame oil
4 teaspoons chilli oil

method

★ Steam the vegetables and leave them to cool, or plunge them into cold water.

★ Whizz the dressing ingredients together in a blender or food processor.

★ Cook and cool the broken noodles.

★ Mix the cooked vegetables with the noodles in a bowl, pour over the dressing and toss the salad.

hiyashi chuka

Cold noodles, Chinese-style, hiyashi chuka is garnished with the type of thinly-sliced preserved ginger that is usually served with sushi. Look for it in Oriental supermarkets.

ingredients

200g ramen noodles, cooked and cooled

for the sauce:
$1^1/2$ dessertspoons light soy sauce
2 dessertspoons mirin
1 dessertspoon rice vinegar
1 teaspoon sesame oil
a few drops of chilli oil
1 teaspoon tahini

for the topping:
30g shredded cucumber
25g shredded carrot
30g shredded cooked chicken
1 crabstick, shredded

to garnish:
sushi ginger
mustard or wasabi

method

★ Arrange the cold noodles on a large plate.

★ Arrange the shredded crabstick, chicken, cucumber and carrots on top of the noodles.

★ Combine the ingredients for the sauce and spoon it over the noodles and topping.

hiyashi chuka

spicy soba salad

way of wagamama

'simplicity is the end of art and the beginning of nature.'

BRUCE LEE

breathing in

Breathing is the most crucial process for the maintenance of life and it is essential that we drink plenty of water. However, at wagamama we believe that eating is the most important activity in our daily lives. Because our eating habits greatly determine the quality and duration of our lives, the quality of the food that we eat, no less than the purity of the air we breathe and the water we drink, is vital.

What we eat shapes our physical health and well-being; the way we eat animates our spirit. Eating should not be merely a mechanical refuelling process. A meal should be a joyous and convivial experience providing not only sustenance for the body but nourishment for the soul.

In London, where wagamama began, eating out has become a way of life for many people. During the 1980s, a decade characterised by economic materialism, eating out at expensive restaurants became the ultimate expression of conspicuous consumption for the era's so-called 'yuppies'. Over the same period, fast food outlets proliferated to cater for the masses. As belts were tightened and corporate expense accounts slashed in the recessionary atmosphere of the early 1990s, it became clear that people were not prepared to sacrifice the habit of eating out. They continue to visit restaurants, only now they demand better value for money. While expensive and formerly fashionable establishments went to the wall, less illustrious places prospered by offering less complicated food in a less reverent atmosphere at more down-to-earth prices.

new values

Around the turn of the Eighties, advertisers began to discern a new mood among potential consumers. A fresh awareness of environmental issues caused a significant proportion of the population to reassess their criteria when choosing what to buy. Nowadays, petrol must be unleaded, detergent has got to be eco-friendly and paper really should be recycled.

Throughout the Eighties the concept of 'lifestyle' was used to sell all sorts of products, from clothes and domestic appliances to magazines, music and food. Consumers selected products that appealed to them through perceived associations of style, quality and status, which were routinely reinforced by cunning advertising campaigns. As the new decade dawned, in line with the new concern for their environment, many people began to question the true worth of goods that were supposed to enhance some ad man's vision of what your lifestyle should be like. They became increasingly suspicious of spurious advertising messages. The conventional view of modern consumers is that they buy things to adorn and express the lifestyle to which they aspire. The assumption is that their choices are more-or-less consistent and recognisable. The reality is far more complex.

Fewer people seek to define themselves through material possessions these days; they are far more likely to pride themselves on being too smart to buy banal products. Rather, their choices are becoming increasingly eclectic and selective, informed by values that were formerly the prerogative of the wealthy and educated, or talented and bohemian, but are now more common.

enter the dolphin

Marketing analysts reckon that the financial constraints of recession, combined with heightened awareness of environmental issues and an increasingly sceptical attitude toward advertising, has produced a new and more sophisticated species of 'post-modern' consumer: meet the dolphin. Dolphins are anti-fashion and they don't want work to dominate their lives. Maybe their biggest worry is the state of the world around them.

The snobbery that attached itself to brand names in the Eighties has been superseded in the Nineties by a modified form of materialism. The remodelled po-mo shopper is not impressed by labels, but more interested in the down-to-earth, honest-to-goodness qualities of the things he or she chooses to buy. Purchasing decisions are made according to often inscrutable criteria that relate to a mosaic of beliefs in the shopper's mind about the integrity of particular products.

To work out if you are a dolphin, close your eyes, hold your breath, and imagine you're in the supermarket, looking to buy a can of tuna. Do you conscientiously search for the words, 'dolphin friendly' on the label? If so, welcome to the wonderful, post modern world of wagamama!

the fast food culture

The term 'fast food' does not refer to a specific product but to an industrialised process in which food is mass-produced in a systematised way that is the philosophical opposite of conventional cooking. The conventional cook prides him or herself on having skill, taste and good judgement, but fast food systems are designed to be operated by unskilled employees, who have minimum knowledge and no experience.

The most significant innovation in the history of fast food service was the reversal of the first rule of traditional hospitality, the personal touch. To ensure the fastest possible service to the customer, fast food is frequently cooked before it is even ordered and kept warm until requested. It might be said that the triumph of the fast food operators has been to persuade paying customers to accept the impersonal touch: 'Have a nice day, next please!'

Fast food is an American invention that has been exported globally, but not always happily. With only minor modifications, the products offered by fast food chains are the same the world over; standardisation is the number one priority and predictability the principal selling point. The products of international burger and pizza chains are consistently good or bad wherever you eat them. This situation may be reassuring for timid consumers, but from the po-mo point of view, it's boring!

the strong wind blows; the bamboo bends

Conceived in an austere economic environment, wagamama was intended to serve the people, who had been patiently waiting for food that is delicious, nutritious and inexpensive. The concept of wagamama grew from the belief that eating out can be egalitarian and convivial, respectful and enjoyable. Not only does wagamama offer value for money in terms of the price you pay at the till, but we also strive to provide an aesthetically-pleasing environment in which to eat.

wagamama is an informal eating place, not a 'proper' restaurant. It is not a self-service canteen,

food orders are
punched into hand-
held electronic pads
and relayed to the
kitchen via a radio
signal...

...where they are
printed out at the
appropriate cooking
station.

swiftly, each order is processed and each dish assembled...

...and despatched as quickly as it is cooked.

nor a cafe. Is wagamama a fast food joint? That depends on your definition.

Like a fast food unit, bookings are not accepted. wagamama has waiter service, rather than expecting customers to order at a counter and find their own seats. wagamama makes full use of the latest technology to speed up the ordering process: orders are keyed into hand-held mobile pads and relayed by a radio signal to the appropriate station in the kitchen. The food is served fast, but every dish is cooked to order. Dishes are delivered to the table as soon as they are ready, so meals do not always arrive at the same time. Wait for your mate and your food will go cold, so eat up!

Like a fast food unit, the kitchen at wagamama is open plan in order to maximise operational efficiency. Cooks and waiters can maintain eye contact and food is served directly over the counter. Customers can see their food being cooked and enjoy the spectacle of the kitchen, where workers scurry to and fro amid great clouds of steam, and fast food systems analysts can ogle our semi-automatic dumpling-making machine.

Noodles are served in attractive, high-quality bowls and eaten with disposable chopsticks. Although the chopsticks are used only once and then thrown away, they are made from a biodegradable and easily renewed material – bamboo – so there is little environmental damage. Nor is there superfluous packaging.

The answer to the conundrum is that wagamama is both a fast food operation and it is not. The most obvious disqualification is the queue. The early popularity of wagamama has meant that it can barely function as originally intended, as a 'non-destination food station', since people have to wait for so long on the stairs to be fed!

form is emptiness; emptiness is form

What makes wagamama so popular, so appealing that people are prepared to wait in the rain, as sometimes they must, just to experience a few moments of wagamagic? This is the question that preoccupies our commercial rivals. One restaurant operator's response was: 'I don't get it! This place is in the middle of nowhere and there is a queue here every day.'

Of course, Bloomsbury is not in the middle of nowhere, but in the heart of London. There are plenty of people around and many of them like to come to eat at wagamama. Perhaps they are all properly-initiated and fully-fledged noodle devotees. Maybe they just like the atmosphere of the place. Or could it be some strange kink in the national psyche that urges the British to form an orderly line outside any place that promises value for money?

The first thing that strikes visitors to wagamama is its purity. A sign over the ashtray at the door indicates that within is a clean air environment and that smoking is not permitted. The interior architecture is simple, functional and uncluttered. Utilitarian, economically-selected materials – ash, steel, marble, render and stainless steel – have been purposefully used in order to reflect the fresh, natural produce that is used in the cooking.

The work of John Pawson, the architect who provided the inspiration for design of the pilot site of wagamama, has been described as 'rigorously sensual minimalism'. Pawson has a profound respect for the idea that less is more. His interiors are characterised by their lack of ornament —

'clutter' as he calls it – and lack of distracting decorative details.

The urge to pare architecture down to its barest elements and thus to simplify our surroundings is an expression of a desire for spiritual purity and renewal. One highfalutin commentator compared the atmosphere of wagamama to a hondo, the refectory of a Zen temple, where the concept of wabi is most perfectly expressed. Wabi means 'voluntary poverty', and refers to the ascetic lifestyle practised by Buddhist monks who reject material possessions in the search for spiritual enlightenment.

The natural materials and earthy colours of the wagamama interior remind our customers of our integrity and concern for their well-being. There is nothing to distract those who choose to eat at wagamama from their food, or each other. People sometimes express surprise that, in the middle of a bustling and busy wagamama, a private conversation with the person sitting opposite you.is perfectly possible. Amid chaos, there is calm.

adopt, adapt and change

From its early success, we can begin to hope that wagamama is an idea whose time has come. Like many good ideas, however, wagamama is not unique. There are plenty of good Vietnamese noodle shops in San Francisco, for instance; we like to go there for the pho! The largest chain of ramen bars in Japan, *Dosanko,* now has eight units in the New York area. In Los Angeles there is an embryonic chain of noodle bars called *Mikoshi,* which was set up around the same time as wagamama by the largest Japanese fast food franchise chain, *MOS.*

In Japan, American-style fast food has been even more prodigiously successful than in Britain. Over the past decades, young people in particular have thrown down their chopsticks and gobbled up countless burgers and pizzas and pieces of fried chicken, all of which are sold there by fast food chains based in the United States.

The largest Japanese fast food chain sells American-style beef patties, modified for domestic tastes with the addition of soy and sugar. By adopting American marketing methods and adapting an American product to suit local requirements, *MOS Food Services* has achieved a dominant position in Japan during a period in which American-style fast food was seen as a potent symbol of cultural change.

When it came to expanding into the USA, *MOS* did not try to compete with American burger chains on their home turf, but came up with their own ramen shop concept, called it *Mikoshi Japanese Noodle House,* and tested it in suburban shopping malls.

According to the operations manager of *Mikoshi,* the concept was unveiled there to a public that had tasted teriyaki, but whose only brush with the mystique of Japanese noodles may have come from obscure screenings of the 1987 cult movie, *Tampopo.* ' From the perspective of most Americans, you mention Japanese food and they automatically think of sushi,' he said, 'but what we've offered them is their first experience of ramen and yaki soba noodles.'

wagamama is a little bastard

The synchronicity of *Mikoshi* with wagamama is an interesting, but ultimately irrelevant coincidence. The two may share common points of reference,

wagamama works

for everyone

but they are fundamentally different. *Mikoshi* is attempting to translate an authentic Japanese ramen house into suburban Californian culture; wagamama wants to adapt and improve the noodle bar, making it more attractive to those who empathise with our ideals of positivity.

Soon after wagamama opened, we received complaints from several aggrieved Japanese expatriots: 'wagamama is not a propitious name for a restaurant!' declared one. 'There are not many Japanese people in the kitchen,' observed another, 'with the result that the ramen does not taste as it should.'

We like this kind of 'how dare you' reaction, because wagamama is not supposed to be an authentic Japanese noodle bar. We are not concerned with tradition for its own sake, nor with cultural purity! We believe that to be a good student is not to reproduce the same recipe as one's teacher, but to adapt it, reflecting the essence of our time and making it better by making it for ourselves and in our own way.

Noodles will always be our business, but we will research and develop new ideas for recipes, wherever we may find them. Being an upstart, with no orthodox background, wagamama is not afraid to make mistakes. And we will employ whoever we like.

The outrage over the idea that a restaurant could be named after a naughty child merely reflects the sterility of the restaurant scene. Japanese establishments have been around since the 1960s, but the insularity of Japanese social structure has meant that the majority of their clients continue to be homesick salarymen with fat corporate expense accounts. In their earnest striving for authenticity,

refined Japanese restaurants have forgotten their obligation to provoke and intrigue, so they have become staid and formal and deadly dull.

Picture it this way: a still pool of water reflects a perfect mirror image, but throw a stone into it and the surface tension is shattered. The harmony of the water has been disturbed and the image distorted. But the rippled reflection is dazzling, more fascinating than before. This condition of localised chaos in the context of universal harmony is a potent concept in Zen and a key to the playful way of wagamama.

if there is no problem, there can be no solution

Kaizen is the guiding principle of wagamama. It's meaning is 'continuous improvement'. There is no equivalent English word, but kaizen is one of the most commonly used expressions in contemporary Japan, where everybody discusses the kaizen of everything from the state of the economy to their personal relationships. Kaizen also refers to the core belief that informs the management techniques that many observers have identified as the key to Japan's contemporary economic success.

Ironically, the philosophy of kaizen is largely derived from ideas of an American academic, a quality-control expert called Dr W. Edwards Deming, who was brought to Japan by General MacArthur to assist in the process of post-war reconstruction. Deming taught that total quality management is not a simple matter of meeting a certain standard but an ongoing process of improvement.

Explaining how to strengthen their manufacturing base in order to compete in the free market, Deming taught the Japanese to adopt the standard motto of many successful businesses: 'every day, in simple ways, strive to be better than the day before'. In the West, many people pay lip service to this idea without appreciating its full significance, but the Japanese took it to heart.

Although the current generation of Japanese teenagers appear to be reacting against their parents' characteristic conformity, individuality has been valued less in Japan than in Britain or America. The Japanese are temperamentally conservative and inclined to be rather reticent; theirs is a consensual culture in which team work flourishes. With their determination to rebuild a shattered economy, the Japanese took on board the lessons Deming taught them, developed the mature management philosophy of kaizen and used it to formulate their game plan for economic success.

Rather than rely on tried and tested production methods, kaizen dictates that companies must always seek to improve the efficiency of their operational systems and the atmosphere of the working environment. Do this and the end product will inevitably be better. Western firms often seem to operate with the maxim, 'if it ain't broke, don't fix it'. Japanese workers are frequently reminded, 'there will be no progress if you keep on doing the same things exactly the same way all the time'.

seeking perfection in an imperfect world

Progress in the West is usually defined in terms of innovation, with manufacturers frequently claiming that the latest exciting new invention will revolutionise our lives. You will wonder how you ever managed to live without it! From the perspective of kaizen, however, change is not such a big deal. Change is an inevitable and continuous

process that happens hour by hour and must be managed moment by moment, because everything is transient. Western management is orientated toward arbitrary goals, setting production targets and rewarding the workforce if those projections are met. But with kaizen the goal is perfection. Since total perfection can never be achieved, there is always room for improvement and never any occasion to feel completely satisfied or complacent.

Rather than being concerned primarily with results, kaizen management is process-orientated: every day, the workers are actively looking for ways to improve the efficiency of existing systems and to make better products. They are rewarded for identifying potential problems as well as proposing workable solutions, not merely for increased productivity.

The concept of perfection is far more prevalent in Oriental thinking than in the West, as is the notion of linear progress without any limit to possible improvement, which is implicit in the practice of Zen Buddhism. This abstract notion is grounded in the understanding that, while striving for complete harmony and perfect understanding, such a state of grace is unobtainable in this life.

walk on

In the final analysis, kaizen is not a fixed set of rules that will automatically result in economic success but a state of mind that informs a strategy for success. Kaizen assumes that to succeed and develop we need to be constantly growing, expanding our awareness and improving the quality of our lives.

More deeply, kaizen assumes that every aspect of our way of life deserves to be constantly improved.

quality assurance
procedures at
wagamama are
hands-on.

the yaki soba
station is perhaps
the hottest job in
the kitchen.

at the end of the day, the wagamama kitchen crew congratulate each other on another day's work well done.

At wagamama, we believe that this optimism is the most important attitude that anyone can adopt and apply to the circumstances of their own lives in order to be happier and more fulfilled. It is in this spirit that we hope readers of this book will approach the recipes.

Remember, as we learned from *Tampopo,* noodle soups are synergistic; every component of the dish demands careful attention, but an understanding of the processes involved in constructing a well-balanced noodle soup is crucial. Therefore, read the recipes and comprehend them, but set them aside before you begin to cook.

the way of wagamama is no way

Bruce Lee is our role model. The legendary martial artist developed his own fighting style, Jeet Kune Do, which has been criticised by many traditionalists for not being pure. In fact, JKD is a mish-mash of fighting forms plundered from many different styles. Bruce Lee's response to his critics was that it does not matter whether a martial art is true to its historical origins. All that matters is the end result.

One must 'reach out and absorb what is useful'. Bruce did not only learn Kung-fu, he studied just about every martial art going. From his early Wing Chun training, Bruce absorbed the best elements of the style and then he moved on. With an open mind he continued to search for the quintessential components of other styles, from which he synthesised the most dynamic and lethal modern fighting art; a brand new style. A new style has no tradition, no cultural context, and no unnecessary etiquette or form.

wagamama is a new style noodle bar that is unique

to London, and not quite like any place in Tokyo. Although our main inspiration comes from Japan, wagamama is a synthesis of ideas and recipes that have been appropriated and adapted from a diverse variety of cultural sources. The wagamama way is to consider everything, but to select only what is most useful.

Cookery, like a martial art, has both physical and spiritual aspects. Via a rigid conventional training, the fighter learns to access the spiritual dimension of his or her art through absolute mastery of the physical movements. Only when a student has practised to the point that he or she is quick and supple enough to sequence these movements spontaneously, unselfconsciously, responding to changing situations instinctively – only then can the fighter begin to really cook!

Bruce Lee was the most gifted martial artist, but he was also the most dedicated. He worked out every day, constantly improving, because nobody knew better than Bruce that fluidity is strength. Jeet Kune Do is defined as 'using no way as way; having no limitation as limitation'.

come in peace; leave in tranquillity

Those who love activity are like lightning in the valley or a guttering candle in the wind. Those who are placid are like dead ashes, or like logs. Certain martial styles are inspired by the belief that one should be like the hawk that hovers in stationary clouds, or like the fish that leaps in still waters. There is action in the midst of stillness, harmony within discord, and silence within noise. With this thought, one enters the mind and body of the way of wagamama.

wagamama is a way of life and a state of mind, both verb and noun. To tell the whole truth, the idea of wagamama sprang wholly-formed, motivated by the following thoughts:

success in life is the result of good judgement
good judgement is the result of experience
and experience is the result of bad judgement
there are no failures
there are only results

the noodle kitchen

The main item of kitchen equipment you will need to make noodle soups is a large stockpot, which can also be used to boil noodles. Use the largest pot you have available. If you wish to buy a brand new pot, look for a stainless steel one with an integral steamer attachment, which will be very useful. Otherwise, bamboo steamer baskets are inexpensive and easily found in Oriental supermarkets.

Woks, too, are generally available. Choose one with a reasonably thick base, a sturdy handle and, if possible, a non-stick finish. If buying a cheap iron wok, make sure you oil it thoroughly and season it over a high heat before use.

To strain your noodles, a long-handled strainer is ideal, but a common or garden colander or a large kitchen sieve will do just as well.

Noodle soups taste better when served in bowls that are deep enough to allow the soup to breathe and the noodles to swim. Choose solid, capacious bowls and also invest in some suitable wooden or porcelain spoons so you can slurp your soup with maximum gusto.

notes on the recipes

All the noodle soup recipes are devised to fill a single bowl, so the quantities must be multiplied by the number of mouths you are intending to feed. At *wagamama*, a portion of fresh uncooked ramen noodles weighs precisely 125g and, because our bowls are big, they swim in 450ml, or nearly half a litre of soup. We believe that it is important to have big bowls, giving the ramen room to breathe.

Unless you have purchased them especially, it is unlikely that your bowls will be quite as large, so we have standardised the soup content of all the recipes at 350ml, but this should be adjusted to suit the size of your own bowls. The noodles should be suspended in the soup, but the toppings must sit on them without becoming saturated. The quintessential example of harmonious balance in a bowl of noodle soup is, perhaps, a correctly served tempura soba. The batter of the tempura should faintly sizzle in the soup, yet retain some crunch.

We acknowledge that not everyone will be able to use fresh noodles all of the time. Dried noodles, frequently sold in 500g packets, are acceptable.

The classic condiment used to season ramen dishes is white pepper. Shichimi togarishi, seven spice mixture, which is usually sold in a small glass bottle with a red or green cap, is also acceptable. Shichimi contains flakes of red pepper, the roughly-ground pods of a special Japanese pepper called sansho, flecks of ground mandarin orange peel, black hemp seeds or white poppy seeds, bits of dark green nori seaweed, and roasted sesame seeds. We aren't too proud of it, but we also like to use Schwartz's pepper onion powder.

Some of the ingredients we refer to in the recipes have different names to indicate slightly different types of the same sort of item, which may cause confusion. For example: naruto and kamaboko are slightly different, but interchangeable types of Japanese fishcake; menma and shinachiku both refer to pickled bamboo shoots; wakame is the type of seaweed most commonly used for soups, but nori is a good substitute.

Dried wakame should be reconstituted by soaking for 15 minutes in cold water and drained thoroughly before use. Dried shiitake mushrooms should be soaked for at least two hours or boiled for a good 15 minutes, until the pungent smell evaporates.

Ramen dishes are usually garnished with spring onions, which can be chopped in two ways: either very finely or 'inch angled', which means in diagonal slices about 3–4cm long. Some noodle cooks insist that it is necessary to wrap the chopped onion in a piece of muslin or the corner of a clean tea towel and to squeeze out the excess water, which will also remove any trace of bitterness. At wagamama we like the true taste of onion and consider this procedure unnecessary. Instead, keep the chopped onion in a bowl of cold water, which will maintain its freshness without impairing the flavour.

more information

If you are intrigued or excited about any of the ideas mentioned in the various chapters of this book and wish to know more, good! Here is a critical selection of the key texts that we have found most useful.

positive eating + positive living

First published in 1984, *Raw Energy* by Leslie Kenton and her daughter, Susannah, is described by its publishers, Ebury Press, as 'the revolutionary bestseller.' This is no hyperbole.

We have also found John and Marilyn Diamond's *Fit for Life* and its successor, *Living Health,* (both published by Bantam) very useful. The Diamonds follow a dietary regime called Natural Hygiene, which is also endorsed by the American personal development expert, Anthony Robbins. His first book, *Unlimited Power*, includes a chapter on nutrition entitled 'Energy: the Fuel of Excellence', which has been an inspiration to wagamama.

Probably the best book explaining the nutritional and ecological principles of the macrobiotic diet is the revised edition of *Macrobiotic Diet* by Michio and Aveline Kushi, published by Japan Publications, Inc. The Kushis are leaders of the international macrobiotic community and founders of One Peaceful World information network; their writing has an evangelical tone and a message that should not be ignored.

East Meets West: Super Nutrition from Japan by Dr Hirotomo Ochi (Ishi Press International) is a useful introduction to the so-called 'superfoods' within the traditional Japanese diet, but to find out all there is to know about soybeans refer to *Nature's Miracle Protein* by Tokuji Watanabe and Asahako Kishi. *Culinary Treasures of Japan* (Avery) is written by John and Jan Belleme who import and distribute a range of Japanese food products in America.

There are many books about juicing on the market, but few are worth the cover price. One of the cheapest and most useful is *The Juicing Detox Diet* by Caroline Wheater, a slim paperback published by Thorsens.

way of the noodle

The video of Juzo Itami's seminal film from 1986, *Tampopo,* is distributed by Electric Pictures and available by mail order for £14.99, plus postage; telephone 071 957 8957 for further details. Described as the 'ultimate food movie,' the story of how the trucker, Goro, teaches the widow, Tampopo, to be a proper noodle cook is intercut with a series of hilarious vignettes, concerning all aspects of the human desire for oral gratification. Trainee geishas learn to eat Italian pasta noiselessly, without slurping. A junior salaryman causes consternation at a plush, Western-style restaurant by not ordering exactly the same as his boss. Another man's insatiable appetite kills his hard-working wife. Most of all, in a parallel universe, a white-suited gourmet gangster enjoys a series of gustatory sex scenes with his mistress, including the infamous eggy kiss.

Japanese cookery books rarely mention ramen, except to dismiss it as a Chinese speciality. Shizo Tsuji's *Japanese Cooking, a Simple Art*, published by Kodansha International, is the most comprehensive book in English on the subject. It includes a useful section on menrui, plus recipes, and an introduction by the late, great American food writer, M F K Fisher, who writes: '...why not a full lunch of fresh, hot udon in good broth, perhaps with some slices of raw mushroom or even a few hapless bay-shrimp turning colour at the bottom? Yes, we can adjust to all this, and we must simplify our cooking just as the Japanese have done, by learning a few more of its complexities, while we still have time.'

Kodansha also publish *The Book of Soba* by James Udesky, which is not only the most authorative, but also about the only book in English about the history and lore surrounding traditional Japanese buckwheat noodles.

Another cookery book we have enjoyed is *Step-by-Step Japanese Cooking* by Lesley Downer & Minoru Yoneda, published by The Apple Press.

way of wagamama

For a typical Westerner, confounded by logic, to truly comprehend Zen is not as easy as reading a book or two, although there are plenty of books on the market. We've found that a couple of the oldest published guides in English to be the most useful. *Zen, a Way of Life* by Christmas Humphries was first published in 1962 and remains an excellent introduction to the subject as a paperback in the Hodder & Stoughton *Teach Yourself* series. Christmas, as we familiarly call him, is particularly useful if used in conjunction with Dr Suzuki's seminal work, *An Introduction to Zen Buddhism*, which was first published in 1949 and is now available in a paperback edition with an introduction by Christmas and a foreword by Carl Jung.

Both these eminent writers would warn against the so-called phenomenon of 'Beat Zen' in which a facile understanding of the way of Zen is used as an excuse for perverse or anti-social behaviour. If all you seek from Zen is a selection of pleasing paradoxes, look no further than *The Book of Zen,*

Freedom of the Mind by Tsai Chih Chung, a comic book published by Asiapac, which illustrates many the classic stories that demonstrate the essential principals if Zen. Asiapac have a range of comic strip interpretations of classic Oriental texts, which also includes the *Sayings of Menicius* and *The Art of War* by Sun Wu.

The Japanisation of British Industry by Nick Oliver and Barry Wilkinson (Blackwell) includes a useful chapter on Japanese Industrial Practice, which includes a discussion of kaizen, but the most comprehensive (and comprehensible) book on the subject is *Kaizen, the Key to Japan's Competitive Success* by Masaaki Imai, published by McGraw Hill.

Antony Robbin's *Unleash the Power Within* (Simon & Schuster) also refers to kaizen in order to help explain how to take immediate control of your mental, emotional, physical and financial destiny. Robbins is one of the great motivators and most spell-binding public speakers of his generation. We take his message seriously!

Bruce Lee's *Tao of Jeet Kune Do* is a collection of the kung-fu master's writing that was published posthumously. Copies can be hard to find, but it's worth looking in martial arts equipment stores. There are many other books about Bruce, but few of them are good. One of the better ones is *Jeet Kune Do; Art and Philosophy of Bruce Lee*, published by Know How Publishing of Los Angeles. To see Bruce in action, of course, one has only to hire the video of one of his movies; *Enter the Dragon* is our favourite.

stockists of ingredients

Some of the ingredients discussed in this book may not be available in your local supermarket, but they are not difficult to locate if you know where to look. Good quality dried Japanese noodles – soba and udon – can often be found in health food stores, where brand names to look out for include *Sanchi* and *Sakurai*. The Sakurai family of Monokamo City has expanded its business to become an international supplier of macrobiotic quality noodles under a range of brand names, including a variety of different types of instant ramen.

Kikkoman, the biggest manufacturer of soy sauce, also markets a range of 25 basic ingredients for Japanese cooking, which are widely available throughout the UK. The *Kikkoman* range includes: udon and soba noodles, kelp and bonito flakes for making dashi, wakame and dried shiitake for garnishing noodles soups, and teriyaki sauce and mirin as well as, of course, soy sauce.

Muji is a Japanese shop with branches in London and Glasgow selling 'no brand goods,' including udon and soba noodles and konbu.

London & South East

Ayame Unit L–13 Gyosei College, Acacia Road, Reading, Berks.
Canterbury Whole Foods 10 The Borough, Canterbury, Kent.
Freshland 196 Old Street, London. EC1
Intel Supermarket 126 Malden Road, New Malden, Surrey.
J A Centre Supermarket 348-356 Regents Park Road, London, N3.
Japan Foods 67 A Camden High Street, London, NW1.
Loon Fung Chinese Supermarket 42-44 Gerrard Street, Chinatown, London, W1.

Wild Oats 210 Westbourne Grove London W11.
Midori 19 Marlborough Place, Brighton.
Miura Foods 40 Coombe Road, Kingston, Surrey.
Muji 26 Great Marlborough Street, London, W1.
Ninjin 244 Great Portland Street, London, W1.
Yaohan Plaza 399 Edgware Road, Collingdale,

South West

Carlrey & Co 36 St Austell St, Truro, Cornwall.
Wild Oats 9–11 Lower Redland Road, Bristol.

East Anglia

Arijuna 12 Mill Road, Cambridge.
Rainbow Wholefoods 14–16 Dove Street, Norwich.

Birmingham

Wing Yip 96–98 Coventry Street, Birmingham.

Manchester

Wing Yip 45 Faulkner Street, Manchester.

Doncaster

Countryside Wholefoods 80 Copley Road, Doncaster.

Newcastle-upon-Tyne

Setsu Japan 196 Heaton Road, Newcastle-upon-Tyne.

Scotland

Muji 63–67 Queen Street, Glasgow.
Sakura Fuji 28 Grasgon Road, Edinburgh.
Real Foods 37 Broughton Street, Edinburgh.

glossary

antioxidants vitamins C, E and A, which are abundant in raw fruits and vegetables

daikon a long white radish

dashi the fundamental cooking stock of Japanese cuisine, made with giant kelp and bonito flakes

enoki a delicate variety of Japanese mushroom

five spice powder a fiery Chinese seasoning mix

hondo the refectory of a Zen Buddhist temple

kaizen gradual, ongoing and simple improvements

kamaboko a type of fishcake (see also naruto and yaki chikura)

katsuo bonito, a fish of the mackerel family, which is dried and shaved into flakes to make dashi (q.v.)

konbu` sometimes also translated as kombu, is a species of seaweed similar to giant kelp, used to make dashi (q.v.)

macrobiotic from the Greek meaning 'long-lived', the practice includes the selection and preparation as well as the manner of cooking and eating food

menma pickled bamboo shoots (see also shinachiku)

menrui the Japanese word for noodles, of which there are four main types: ramen, soba, udon and somen (q.v.)

mirin sweet sake used for cooking

miso a paste made from fermented soya beans

mouli a radish-like vegetable, like daikon

naruto Japanese fishcakes (see also kamaboko)

nori the type of seaweed used to wrap sushi and to garnish noodle soups

ramen Chinese–style noodles; one of Japan's most popular fast foods

shichimi togarashi seven spice red pepper, an excellent seasoning for ramen

shinachiku pickled bamboo shoots (see also menma)

shiitake a robust, almost meaty variety of Japanese mushroom

shojin the devotional cuisine served in Zen Buddhist temples

shoyu naturally-made Japanese soy sauce

soba traditional Japanese noodles made with buckwheat flour

somen fine white noodles like vermicelli

tamari strong, sweetish, wheat-free soy sauce

teriyaki sauce a mixture of soy sauce, sake, mirin and sugar

te'uchi made by hand

tofu bean curd made from soaked, mashed and strained soya beans

udon thick white noodles made from wheatflour

wabi the Buddhist practice of voluntary poverty

wakame a species of seaweed with long green fronds and a silky texture that is often used in soups

wasabi green Japanese horseradish paste, often sold as a powder

yaki chikura a type of fishcake similar to naruto and kamaboko, used in pan-fried dishes

yin/yang the opposing but complementary forces of nature characterised as dark and light, male and female, acid and alkali

wagamama is...

childlike, not childish

unsophisticated and unadulterated

impatient but playful

constantly exploring

always asking questions

getting ever better

innocent, honest